A

Ki heard the shotgun click behind him and he knew he could do nothing in time to save his own life. He flung himself to the ground, rolling, waiting for the inevitable thunderblast, the hot spray of deadly pellets.

But it didn't come.

Sitting up, Ki looked in amazement at the man with the shotgun who had dropped his weapon and was slapping his back for some reason. When he turned Ki saw why.

A *tonti,* a throwing knife, was imbedded in his spine. As Ki watched, the man toppled forward face first and hit the alley floor to lie there unmoving, dead.

And the Master emerged from the shadows . . . He wore a gold robe with flaring sleeves. His white hair was knotted at the back of his narrow skull. Arched white eyebrows sheltered penetrating dark eyes.

"First you would kill me," Ki said, "and then you would save my life. Which is it you have come to do?"

"To kill you, of course," Kobi-san answered softly.

— WESLEY ELLIS —

LONE STAR

AND THE
MASTER OF DEATH

JOVE BOOKS, NEW YORK

LONE STAR AND THE MASTER OF DEATH

A Jove Book / published by arrangement with
the author

PRINTING HISTORY
Jove edition / February 1988

ISBN: 0-515-09446-3

Jove Books are published by The Berkley Publishing Group,
200 Madison Avenue, New York, New York 10016.
The name "JOVE" and the "J" logo
are trademarks belonging to Jove Publications, Inc.

PRINTED IN THE UNITED STATES OF AMERICA

10 9 8 7 6 5 4 3 2 1

Chapter 1

"How far?"

Ki looked at the lovely honey-blond woman beside him and then up the long trail toward the Rocky Mountains of Colorado, which stood dark and forbidding, wreathed with dark clouds. A cold wind gusted out of the north, folding the long grass on either side of the rutted road in front of them.

"Ten miles?" Ki guessed with a shrug. His horse blew and he steadied it with a hand on its neck. "You haven't been to Beaverton?"

"No." Jessica Starbuck removed her flat-crowned hat and swept back her hair. "I had to go through the books to make sure we even owned the Centennial Mine. We do, through a subsidiary company."

Ki just nodded. The Japanese-American understood very well, although most people wouldn't have, how a lady from Texas could own a rich silver mine in Colorado and not even know it. Jessica Starbuck's father had built a far-flung empire, and he had been wealthy almost beyond estimate. It had taken a tribe of lawyers to straighten things out after Alex Starbuck had been murdered. Jessica's holdings were as rich and vast as the heart which beat beneath her perfectly formed breasts. She had no need for more money. Her life was devoted now to using what she had properly.

If there was law between the Mississippi and the Pacific it was spread thin, and was usually untrustworthy and parochial. There was a need for someone to fill that vacuum:

Jessica Starbuck and her friend, trail companion, and protector, Ki.

"So long as we get in before dark," Jessie said, adjusting the drawstring on her hat. "I can't spend another night on the ground."

"No," Ki agreed. It had been cold, very cold, as they had climbed to the higher elevations. The railroad spur which existed on the Colorado-Union maps was totally imaginary. They had purchased horses at the town of Desolation, and had continued on toward Beaverton, a booming silver camp where Ki hoped, warily, to meet his past.

They walked their horses on, the wind growing colder yet, shifting the manes and tails of their mounts. Ahead, the peaks lay in scrambled confusion, dark clouds nestled in the valleys between the blue peaks of the Rockies.

It was, Ki thought, an unlikely place for a man of the Orient to collide with his past.

The wire from Earl Gibbons in Beaverton had been tantalizing if incredible. Gibbons ran the freight line out of Beaverton, but in the old days he had ridden herd on Lone Star beef. He was a good cowhand, but was too ambitious to stick to droving. With Alex Starbuck's help he had gone into business with two wagons and two mule teams. He knew Jessica and Ki, luckily for the girl who was looking for Ki.

"Gibbons?" Ki's forehead had furrowed at first and then cleared as he remembered the lean cowboy. "What in the world would he be wiring me for?"

"You could open it and find out," Jessica had suggested with a smile.

Ki did, standing before the huge fireplace at the Starbuck ranch to read it. He read it once and then read it again. It was a long wire and his face took on a dozen different expressions as he worked his way through it.

"Yoshiko," he said at last.

"Pardon me?" Jessica was puzzled.

Ki lowered the wire and shook his head, staring into the fire for a long minute before answering, "Someone I knew."

"A secret lover," Jessica teased, but she got no answering smile from Ki.

Ki's mind was in a distant place: the monastery where fog crept along the flagstone paths among the stunted trees, and men walked in silence while others chanted in the temple.

Ki himself, deep in meditation, hadn't seen the young woman emerge from the shrubbery to fall in beside him. When he did notice her it was more of a feeling than a reaction to his senses.

"Yoshiko?" The tall man stopped and turned toward her. The small woman—barely five feet tall—smiled and came to stand in front of him, her eyes sparkling.

"I would walk with you, Ki," she said, touching his arm.

"No. It is not proper," Ki answered.

"But why not?"

"Because you are too young, and because your father and grandfather forbid it," Ki answered, gently removing her hand. "How old are you, fifteen?"

"What does it matter to the heart?" Yoshiko asked. She was a bright-eyed thing, Ki thought; still unformed, with the eager smile of youth and youth's ignorance. Ki, who had come to this place to study under the Master, to hone his martial-arts skills under the great one, had no wish to dishonor his host—and no wish to take on a lover who had somehow become infatuated with him.

"Wait until the proper time," he advised her. "Find someone of your own rank, someone your family might approve of."

"There is no one like you, Ki," Yoshiko had insisted. She was silent as a pair of praying monks walked past. "None so tall, strong, unique."

"There will be others. Younger. Ones who do not have trouble following as a shadow."

"What is it that happened, Ki?" Yoshiko whispered. "They say you are an outlaw." Her voice made it clear that this too made Ki romantic.

Ki just shook his head. He didn't wish to go into that

3

now. He was trying very hard to escape his bloody past. "I am," he said, reaching for an argument that might discourage the girl, "half white. My father was an American merchant."

Yoshiko didn't even answer. Her eyes still glowed. Each argument Ki tried to raise only made him more mysterious and exotic to her. There was one final, substantial argument which sent her scurrying away.

"He is watching. Your grandfather, my master, Kobi-san, is on the balcony," Ki told her. "I have come under his roof and into his school. I will not dishonor him by dallying longer."

Yoshiko turned and looked upward. He was there—the old one in his golden robe, his white hair tied back in a samurai knot. Whether he was looking at them or not she didn't know, but it sent her dashing away...

...But not before she whispered, "I love you, Ki. I always shall. If you stay I shall continue to love you; if you go I shall follow you wherever you go. Do not forget me."

Abruptly she lifted his hand, kissed it, and then ran away into the night, leaving Ki to glance again at the balcony and then walk on through the foggy night.

Jessica Starbuck stretched and reached for her coffee, sipping it as Ki finished speaking, thinking perhaps of many things he didn't wish to discuss then.

"She was only a child," Jessie said at last.

"Yes, but an impetuous one. A persistent one."

"What happened, Ki?"

"Eventually Kobi-san confronted me. The Master was not happy. Who could blame him? Yet he was a restrained man, as a master of the arts must be. He was over sixty then, yet he could have crushed me with one hand."

"*You?*" Jessica laughed. *Ki,* who was the match of six ordinary men, strong and quick and skilled? The man who knew *te*—the art of barehanded combat—well enough to have defeated the worst thugs in the West?

"Yes." Ki was quite serious. "Me. Kobi-san was my teacher; yet I was not taught all he knew. He had spent a

4

lifetime learning. I was still a young man. Then . . . I went away."

"Because of Yoshiko?"

"The young girl did not help," Ki said evasively. Jessica just nodded. Ki was frequently vague about that phase of his life, that time when he had been outlawed. He had been forced to flee to America to search for Alex Starbuck, who had been his own father's friend, and was eventually hired as a bodyguard and protector for Starbuck's beautiful young daughter.

Jessica put her coffee cup down and looked at the dwindling fire herself. A Mexican servant came in and added a log and Jessie thanked him.

When the man was gone, Jessica said, "What can Yoshiko and Gibbons possibly have in common?"

"Nothing, apparently. Earl just says that a Japanese named Yoshiko has been looking for a man named Ki. 'Can it possibly be the same Ki I know? The girl looks so forlorn and helpless that I've taken this long-shot to wire and ask.'"

"You think it is her, Ki?"

"I don't know. It makes no sense, and yet I have this feeling that it may be. At least I feel that I owe it to her to go out to Colorado and find out."

"We will go, then," Jessie had answered.

"There's no point in you making the trip, Jessica. This is not your obligation, but mine."

"I've just said I'm going, Ki," Jessica had replied. Ki gave up arguing. He had spent much time trying to talk Jessica Starbuck out of matters she had made up her mind about, and never with much success. She was her own woman, this strong-willed daughter of Alex Starbuck.

Looking into matters, Jessica had discovered that she owned the Centennial Mine in Beaverton and that it was doing very well indeed. Another interesting fact was brought to her attention. Centennial had a large Japanese labor force. Chinese laborers she might have expected, but this was unusual—and it lent some weight to the possibil-

5

ity that Ki's Yoshiko might somehow have come to this country with a group of immigrants.

Ki didn't like that notion, however. "A girl from a prominent family does not run away to a foreign land to labor in the mines."

"Maybe a woman in love would," Jessica said.

"It is preposterous. The creature is only a child."

"Maybe not in her own mind, Ki. Besides, it's been years since you've seen her."

Ki's face tightened. It was obvious he didn't want anything to do with this, yet he felt a sense of obligation too powerful to ignore. They would go.

What else was there to do?

Now, as they approached Beaverton, the sky was a patchwork of deep purple and burnt orange above the mountain community. The road through the heart of town was rutted and muddy. The saloons were ablaze with light, alive with sound. From higher up the slopes, teams of mules drew wagonloads of miners home from the shafts bored into the mountains. On the higher peaks there was snow. The wind was very cold. Breath rose in clouds from their horses' nostrils as Ki and Jessica swung down in front of the town's only hotel, a three-storied red building with white railings around the porch and balconies.

Jessica, bundled in her long coat, still drew stares as they crossed the lobby. There weren't many women like this one to be found in the far mining camps.

"Yes, sir?" the desk clerk looked up and blinked. The blink became a frown as he studied Ki.

"Two rooms, please. I don't know for how long," Jessica said.

The desk clerk's frown faded into an indefinite, tight expression and he turned the book toward them. As Jessica signed her name she asked, "Can you tell me where I can find Earl Gibbons?"

"The freight-line boss?"

"Yes, that's right."

The clerk shrugged again. "The office, I guess. The

trouble they've been having Gibbons doesn't stray far from there."

"What sort of trouble?" Ki asked.

"Mister, there's silver coming out of the Centennial by the ton. Gibbons freights it out of here. Sometimes it makes it, sometimes it doesn't."

"Where is his office?" Jessica wanted to know.

"Two blocks up, turn right. Consolidated Freight, he calls his outfit."

After getting settled in their small rooms Jessica and Ki walked toward Gibbons's office. The night had gotten cold enough so that there was frost on the muddy street that crackled underfoot as they walked. Now and then a miner staggered past, or someone owlhooted in a saloon, but for the most part Beaverton was silent.

It didn't take much to find the office of Consolidated Freight. A light was burning in a back window and they rapped on the door, hearing heavy footsteps approaching, someone muttering under his breath.

When the door opened Gibbons himself was standing there, tall, hawk-nosed, with thinning gray hair. It took him a minute, peering out into the darkness, to figure out who they were. Then the wary look on his face was replaced by a huge grin.

"Damn all! Jessica Starbuck and Ki. I was wondering if you might show up one day. Come in, please, come in."

As they entered the office Ki noticed that Gibbons had been holding a pistol beside his leg. Now, sheepishly, the freighter holstered it. "There's been a few night visitors I wasn't so glad to see," Gibbons apologized, leading them across the dim outer office to his brightly lit private sanctum, where two coal-oil lamps hung from the wall and a desk cluttered with bills of lading and account books sat in the center of a bare floor.

"What's been going on around here, Earl?" Ki asked.

"With me? Just what you'd expect. I'm shipping silver, Ki. Men want it and they'll use guns to take it. Trouble is, I've kind of extended myself, and if I happen to lose this contract I'm in real trouble."

7

"You won't lose it," Jessica said. "Are you forgetting who owns Centennial?"

Gibbons rubbed his head. "I guess I was forgetting," he answered with a smile. That made him feel better, enough to reach for the bottle in his desk drawer and pour himself a glass of whisky. After a minute the gloom returned.

Gibbons said, "Still, there's no way I can let things go on as they are. Miners are losing their pay. Good men are being killed. Wagons wrecked . . . but then you didn't come here to talk about my troubles, did you?"

"Your troubles are mine, it seems," Jessica answered. "That's Starbuck silver we're talking about, after all."

"Yes it is. But I know you and Ki didn't come this far to go into that just now. It's the Japanese girl, isn't it?"

"That's right. Where is she now, Earl?"

Gibbons shook his head. "Damned if I know. For a time I saw her most every day wandering up and down the street, talking to Japanese and Americans alike. Her question was always the same, 'Do you know a man named Ki?' "

"What did she look like?" Ki asked.

"Short. Pretty Japanese."

That didn't narrow things down very much. Jessica asked, "But you haven't seen her lately?"

"No. Maybe the Japanese community could tell you. Ki, speaking the language, might be able to get somewhere. If I'd tried—which I didn't—I don't think they would have told me a damn thing."

"Trouble there too?" Jessie asked.

"Well . . ." Earl spread his hands. "Strangfeld doesn't seem to do much to make their life any easier up at Centennial. I hear he doesn't pay them right, doesn't see that they're provided with proper chow and housing. I dunno, really. I run their ore but I don't want to get tangled up in Strangfeld's problems."

"He's the mine manager?" Jessie asked.

"That's right. He's big, bluff, raw. Far as I know he's square with everyone in town, but like I say, you hear that the Japanese have a grudge against him. Maybe it's so. It

8

wouldn't be hard to put pressure on those people: 'If you don't like it, go home.' You know."

"If that's what's happening I'll straighten it out," Jessica promised.

"Hope you can," Gibbons said. "Hope you can find that Yoshiko woman too—right one or not. And," he said with a sigh, "as long as you two are at it, I wish you could find a way to break up the outlaws who've been hitting my freighters."

"Anything else?" Jessica asked with a smile. Gibbons smiled in return.

"Not at the moment."

He stood and returned to the door with them after a half an hour's conversation about the old days. Outside, it was dead quiet, dark, the stars bright.

The bullets from the alley across the street sprayed the wooden wall of the freight office and the silent night became a violent bloody spectacle.

Chapter 2

Ki's first move was toward Jessica. He dove toward her, taking her to the ground. From the corner of his eye Ki saw Gibbons stagger backward into the office, clutching his shoulder as his own pistol answered the fire from across the street.

Jessica rolled to one side and got up on one knee behind a water barrel, drawing her own double-action Colt. Bullets ripped huge splinters from the wall behind Ki.

There were two ways for the samurai to go—forward or back. Neither seemed safer than the other. With Jessica's cries ringing in his ears Ki started across the road in a crouch, moving in a zigzag pattern as the snipers' rifles dug up earth at his heels.

Reaching the far side of the street, Ki threw himself into a roll as a Winchester spat flame nearly in his face. The bullet whipped past Ki's head so near that he could hear the whine of it as it passed.

The gunman reared up from behind a packing crate and sighted down the barrel. From across the street Jessica—or Gibbons—sent a bullet smashing into the sniper's face, ripping the man's skull open like a ripe melon as it exited.

Then there was the sound of shouting up the street, and the rapid sounds of feet retreating in the alley. Ki leaped to his feet to pursue the thugs, but by the time he reached the foot of the alley they were lost in the darkness of the Colorado night.

Ki jogged back to where the dead man lay. A crowd had gathered around the body. Jessica was there, unharmed.

"Earl?" Ki asked.

"In the shoulder. Might have broken the collarbone. Someone's gone for the doctor."

A man with a drooping red mustache and a badge on his coat stood up and looked around the circle of onlookers until he spotted Jessie and Ki. His face tightened into a frown.

"You two know anything about this?"

"I do," Jessica said. "I shot him." She stepped in front of Ki to face the town marshal.

"You did?" He looked the beautiful blonde up and down, his eyes coming to rest on the holstered Colt visible beneath her open coat.

"They were after Earl Gibbons. Tried to kill him from ambush."

The marshall glanced toward Gibbons's lighted office and then toed the body over. "Anyone know this man?"

Everyone had a look. He wasn't very pretty just then, and one man turned away to be sick. No one could identify him, but then the marshal hadn't expected any such luck.

"There were two others," Ki volunteered. "They escaped up that alley."

The marshal looked at Ki more closely now. There had been a lot of Japanese in Centennial since the mine hit it big and Mike Strangfeld had started bringing them in, but this one puzzled the marshal. Was he Japanese or not? He was too damn tall for one thing. The man was enigmatic; apparently powerful physically, with the grace of a cat.

"I have to ask you who you two are," the marshal said.

"I am Jessica Starbuck," the lady said, "and this is my friend, Ki."

"Starbuck?" Something rattled around in the back of the marshal's mind and solidified. "Wait a minute—there's a company called Starbuck Enterprises that owns Centennial."

"That's right," Jessica said.

The marshal shook his head. "You sure they were after Gibbons, young woman?"

"Of course. We stepped out the door with Earl and they opened up on us."

11

"That's not what I mean," the marshal persisted. "I'm asking if you know for sure that Gibbons was the intended target. There's a hell of a lot of people who have a grudge against Centennial and the Starbuck company. A chance to get even with the owner of Centennial might be too much for someone to resist."

That was a possibility that Jessica hadn't considered in the heat of the gun-battle. Now she did, soberly.

"It's that bad up there?" Jessica asked. The marshal only shrugged.

"It's out of the town's jurisdiction. All I know is what's rumored."

As Earl Gibbons did.

"They say," the marshall went on with reluctance, "that the Japs are real unhappy with Mike Strangfeld, mad enough to kill. I don't know why they wouldn't feel the same about the owner of the mine."

Ki was crouched over the dead man. "This one," he pointed out, "is hardly Japanese."

"No," the marshal had to agree, "he isn't. But everyone up there ain't Japanese either. Just a guess." The man took a deep breath. "I suppose this is another one I'll never get to the bottom of. Seems like that's the only kind I get lately. Charlie! Get a wagon and cart this body away."

"Marshal," Jessica said, "when you have the time I'd like to talk to you about the situation around here."

"Tonight?" He glanced at a big silver watch.

"If possible."

"I suppose I'll be up for another couple of hours. There's paperwork involved in a gunshot death even in Beaverton, and I have to close down the Empire Saloon. Come by in an hour or so if you want. In any event," he added, "don't leave town, will you?"

"No." Jessica smiled. "We won't leave town."

Their next stop was at Gibbons's bullet-riddled office.

He was on a cot in the outer office. The doctor was just finishing up. A worried-looking, small man with pince-nez glasses, he had bandaged Gibbons's chest tightly and had fashioned a sling. Gibbon's eyes were glazed; his face revealed pain.

A squat, red-headed man, hat in hands, eyed Ki and Jessica suspiciously as they entered and crossed the room.

"How does it look, Doctor?" Jessica asked.

"Dangerous," the doctor said frankly. "I'm going to plug him full of morphine in just a minute. Someone's going to have to make sure he stays on his back for a while—and I mean it, Earl."

"All right." Gibbons's voice was hoarse. He was too beat up to argue just then. "Jessie, Ki, this is Jack Taylor, my foreman."

The red-headed man just nodded to them. "Glad to meet you," Jessie said. "You'll be running things for a time, then?"

"I guess so," Taylor said hesitantly, as if the idea of that responsibility was less than pleasurable.

"You can handle it, Jack," Gibbons said. The doctor was counting out morphine tablets. Earl watched him unhappily.

"I know it, boss. It's the numbers, you know. I can't tote. I never went to school, you know."

Jessica glanced at Ki. What else was there to do? "I'll give you a hand with the books if you like, Earl."

"I'd be grateful. Awful grateful," Earl replied. The doctor handed him half a dozen tablets and a glass of water. It didn't take long before the pills and the lack of blood combined to knock Earl out. The doctor shooed them from the office. A small Mexican woman had been summoned from somewhere, and she pulled up a chair next to Earl's cot.

Outside, Taylor thanked Jessica again. Putting on his hat he added, "I guess I'll stay around tonight. They tried once; they may try again."

As Jessica and Ki stepped off the plankwalk and started toward the marshal's office, Ki said, "It didn't take long for things to get complicated, did it?"

"No. I suppose I shouldn't have offered to do his books, Ki. I'm sorry."

"Sorry? For being generous? That poor teamster, Taylor, was worried sick. What can we do, let Earl's business go under?"

"No. Definitely not. But now we've got his freight line to worry about, along with whatever is going on up at the Centennial. We haven't even begun trying to find Yoshiko."

"If she is here. Yoshiko is a common name."

"Yes." Jessica sounded distracted suddenly.

"What is it, Jessie?"

"I was just thinking about what the marshal said—that maybe those shots weren't intended for Gibbons at all, but for us."

"It seems unlikely. We just arrived tonight. Someone would have to have a pretty good intelligence network."

"Not necessarily, Ki. In a town this size everyone knows what's going on. Maybe Earl talked about us. Or maybe the telegrapher mentioned to a pal that he'd sent a wire to Texas. At any rate, in the morning we're going up to the mine and find out exactly what is going on."

The marshal wasn't back yet and they had to wait around in the cold until he came shambling toward them, head bent away from the cold, gusting wind, and opened the door.

"Nearly forgot about you two. Sorry. Had a shooting at the Empire."

"Busy town you've got here," Ki said as they entered the small office, which was papered with Wanted posters.

"Tell me." The marshal lit a lantern and sat at his desk, taking a flat bottle of whisky from a drawer. "You know how it is," he said between swallows. "A thousand single men with nothing to do but drink cheap liquor."

"What about the Japanese?" Ki asked.

"What do you mean?" The marshal wiped his mouth and poked the bottle away again.

"I can't imagine they sit around the saloons drinking whisky."

"No. They've got their own section of town, the north end. It may be they don't drink whisky, but they know what *sake's* for, and on Saturday night there isn't a hell of

14

a lot of difference between this end of town and that—except they got a few women of their own with them, which slows things down just a little."

"I see. Do the women work?" Ki asked.

"Sure do. Right beside the men in the mine, most of 'em. A few do laundry, cleaning, and such." The marshal paused. "Getting back to the main point," he said, drumming his fingers on his scarred desk top, "you two don't know something you haven't told me about the shooting tonight, do you?"

"Nothing. We talked to Earl for a while, walked to the door with him, and they opened up."

"Talked to him about what?"

"We came to Beaverton to look for someone, a Japanese woman. Earl thought she was here, but now she seems to have vanished."

"I see. He talk to you about his freight business?"

"Naturally."

"Those robberies are something I can't crack. I don't like it, but it doesn't look like I ever will unless I get lucky. I got one deputy, Charlie, and he's just about useless. The bandits, whoever they are, seem to know every move Earl is going to make, which route he's taking, if a wagon's a decoy or the real thing."

"Someone on the inside is giving information?" Jessica asked.

"Seems that way. Inside Earl's outfit or inside the mine."

"Who is this Mike Strangfeld?" Jessica asked.

The marshal looked surprised. "Don't you know? I thought he worked for you."

There was no point in trying to explain the vastness of the Starbuck empire and the fact that as complicated as it was no single person at the top could know every employee personally. Strangfeld must have been hired by another man Jessica barely new, Abel Pearson, who was in charge of Western Development & Exploration, a multi-armed subsidiary.

Jessica just said, "I've never met him, but I intend to. Soon."

"All right," the marshal said, rubbing his eyes wearily. "I suppose that's all there is for tonight. Anything else comes up . . . You're at the hotel?"

"That's right." Jessica and Ki rose to leave. The marshal had one parting thought at the door.

"There's locks on those hotel room doors. You might be sure you use them."

Morning was bright and cool. Jessica had an appetite, and did justice to the hotcakes and eggs they served in the hotel dining room. Ki, ordering only tea and toast, was distracted as he ate. He was in Japan again, seeing the small woman in the garden, the Master on his balcony. He ate only half of his toast before pushing it away.

"What is the plan for this morning?" he asked Jessie.

"I'm going to the mine. You can come along or start doing what you came here to do, Ki."

"Yoshiko. That can wait."

"Can it? The woman's missing and no one seems to know where she's gone. You don't have to go along with me, Ki. I'll be all right."

Ki hesitated, but answered, "All right. If you're sure you won't need me. I want to talk to the people at the north end of town. The marshal said there are laundries, other small businesses. I'll inquire there."

"Then it's settled. I'll ride out to the Centennial. I want to talk to this Strangfeld and find out just what's going on with the Japanese workers."

"You won't forget, Jessica? Someone out there, perhaps Strangfeld, has very possibly been feeding information to the bandits who've been hitting Earl."

"I haven't forgotten. I'll stop in and check on Earl before I go up there, as a matter of fact. See if he has any more definite ideas on who might be doing it."

"He may not even be able to talk this morning. The doctor gave him enough morphine for a horse."

"Maybe not. I want to see how he is anyway. I'll talk to

16

Jack Taylor, if he's around, maybe take a look at Earl's books."

Ki nodded, listening without listening. He had his own work for that day. Yoshiko. He might have convinced Jessica that he wasn't sure it was *her*. But in the back of his mind, he knew. He knew. She was here somewhere, and in trouble. Why else had she vanished from sight?

They took the time to scout around the town on horseback for half an hour or so, wanting to get the general layout. There wasn't much to see. The main drag, three cross streets. At the north end of the main road, jumbled Japanese shanties crowded together. Further up, the road widened again and let up the denuded slope to Centennial.

"I'll leave you here, I guess," Jessica said. "I want to check in at the freight office. Ki." She smiled and touched his hand. "Good luck."

Ki nodded and watched as Jessie turned her horse back toward town. *Good luck*. He figured to need it.

Too many questions remained unanswered. Was it possible that a young and foolish girl had actually traveled halfway around the world out of some romantic whim? And where was she now? Beaverton didn't seem to be an easy place to get lost in.

Ki left his horse at a tiny stable and started his search.

Jessica rode to the freight office and swung down. A wagon was being loaded at the dock in the alley, but it wasn't a silver shipment this time, just wire for the down-country ranchers who were already beginning to string fences across Colorado.

Jack Taylor looked harried and angry. He was staring from one piece of paper to another while an impatient driver watched. Jessica walked around the corner of the counter and smiled at Taylor, who shrugged.

"Something's wrong, but it beats me what," the foreman said. "Wish Earl was on his feet."

"How's he doing?" Jessica asked.

"Still sleeping. He seems okay."

"Jack . . ." the waiting driver interrupted. "I'm short a keg of staples."

"You're supposed to have 'em," Taylor said, rubbing at his corrugated forehead, looking hopefully to Jessica, who was scanning the bill of lading and the inventory sheet which was supposed to match it.

"What is 'Dawkins's'?" Jessica asked, looking up.

"Dawkins's—little mountain saloon. Why?"

"I think a couple of numbers may have been transposed."

"Trans . . ."

"Switched around. It looks like the saloon may have gotten a keg of fence staples instead of a keg of whisky. You might check in the warehouse and see if there's a barrel of whisky out there."

"Dawkins's is on the way if that's it," the teamster said, putting on his hat. He snatched up the bill of lading and went out.

Jack Taylor muttered, "I should've been able to figure that one out."

"It doesn't matter, does it? It's figured out now." There was no one else in the office just then, so Jessica asked, "These bandits that hit the silver shipments, just where do they usually hit?"

"No 'usually' about it," Taylor said, perching on the counter. "They pick a new spot each time. Don't matter which route we use. Thing is, there's only two really good roads out of Beaverton and a smart hombre could sit a hilltop with a set of field glasses and see the wagon coming every time."

"You think that's what's happening?"

"No," Taylor said hesitantly. "Maybe you ought to talk to Marshall King."

"I have. He thinks the outlaws have inside knowledge."

"So it seems." Taylor nodded.

"Any idea who it could be?"

"Hell, no!" Taylor said, flaring up. "And it's not anyone from this office, I'll promise you that. I'd poke around up at Centennial if I was you."

"I intend to," Jessica replied quietly.

18

A voice from behind her said, "Doing my work for me are you, little lady?"

Jessie slowly turned, not liking the 'little lady' business much. A tall man with a dark suit and an infuriating grin was leaning against the doorframe, his hat tugged down rakishly. He was thirty or so, well set up, with a lean face which was clean-shaven and tanned.

"Who are you?" Jessica asked.

The man leaned away from the doorframe and moved toward her with a long, graceful gait. He was taller than Jessica had thought, Ki's size. He removed his hat and grinned down at Jessica.

"Dancer. Michael Dancer."

"That's fine, Mr. Dancer. Happy to know you. Why did you tell me I was doing your work for you?"

"The company's sent me down here," he explained. "Western Development and Exploration. The name wouldn't mean anything to you, but we own Centennial Mines."

"I see. You're some sort of investigator?"

"That's right," the tall man answered. "There's a lot of money being lost in this operation and I'm here to find out why."

Dancer was still grinning, and Jessica felt her cheeks burning. It was the humor in his eyes more than the frank way he appraised her body that annoyed her; after all, she was used to drawing men's eyes. She wasn't, however, used to being mocked.

"All I can do is wish you luck," Jessie said coldly.

"It'll be easier if I can keep the amateurs out of my way," Dancer replied.

That was enough for Jessica. She adjusted her hat and started toward the door. On her way out she paused to turn back toward Taylor.

"Goodbye, Jack. Thank you for talking to me."

"And thank you for your help, Miss Starbuck."

Then Jessica was gone and Dancer, standing staring at the empty doorway, said, "I thought you said *Starbuck*."

"That's what I said. That's Jessica Starbuck."

19

It was another long moment before Dancer's grin returned. He threw back his head and laughed out loud. "That figures. Dancer's luck." He laughed again and then asked Taylor, "You mind going over what you know one more time?"

Outside it was cold with a gusting wind, but Jessica's cheeks still burned. She didn't like Michael Dancer at all. And yet as she swung aboard her horse she smiled, glancing back toward the freight office.

"Hell of a good-looking rascal," she said to the horse. Then she kneed the animal forward, riding out of town toward Centennial on the slopes above.

Riding through the Japanese shanties she looked around for Ki, but he was nowhere to be seen. There wasn't any point in searching for him. He had his own work to do.

The wind was directly in her face as she rode upward through the scattered pines lining the road, and she kept her head bowed so that she never saw where the shot came from. But suddenly her horse was down, and Jessica, pawing at her Colt, was racing for the timber, bullets dogging her heels.

Chapter 3

Jessica dove behind a fallen pine as bullets clipped bark just beside her head. She had her double-action Colt out now, and the slate-gray .38 spoke in response to the guns from across the road. The doomed bay horse lay on the ground, hoofs flailing at the earth in its death run.

The shooting stopped as suddenly as it had begun. Jessica thumbed fresh loads into the cylinder of the .38, hearing the horse's whickering grow lower and then stop. Then there was the sound of birds again, and she heard distantly a horse being ridden away.

Still, Jessica didn't rise from behind the shelter of the dead log. Her eyes searched the forest beyond the road, lifting once to the mine buildings, barely visible higher up the smoke-gray mountain.

There was only the sound of wind, then the cawing of a circling crow. It took Jessie a moment to figure what was wrong: the birds had stopped singing again.

A boot snapped a twig behind her and she rolled onto her back, firing just as a bearded man in a checked red coat leaped toward her, knife in hand.

The .38 bullet drilled its way through his tiny black eyes and made mush of the brain behind them. He fell at Jessica's feet, still trying to clutch at her, although he was already dead.

Jessica's own hand was trembling slightly. That had been just too close. Watching the woods still, she eased away from the body and backed toward the road.

There didn't seem to be anyone else around, but there had been two of them; she was certain of that. It was possible the one she had killed had remained behind afoot while the other rode off, hoping to instill a false sense of confidence in Jessica.

It hadn't quite worked.

Jessica glanced at the dead horse again and crossed the road, working her way up through the timber. The gun was still in her hand. There was no rule against trying twice.

Someone wanted her dead, but who? It seemed it had to be connected with Centennial and the robberies of the silver shipments. Someone didn't appear to want her poking around. This Strangfeld? The mine manager was high on Jessica's list already, and she hadn't yet met him.

Half an hour later she did.

Jessica tramped through the main gate of the Centennial Mine Company and across the muddy yard toward the building where the "Office" sign hung. Men stopped what they were doing and turned wistfully toward her.

Inside, a balding clerk in a scruffy twill suit and dingy white shirt looked up, did a double take, and let his jaw hang for a moment before asking, "May I help you?"

"I'm here to see Mr. Strangfeld."

"He's busy just now. If you could wait, I'll tell him he has a visitor." The clerk rose, his chair scraping the floor. "Who shall I say is calling?"

"Jessica Starbuck."

The clerk's jaw dropped again. He backed away into the inner office, where Jessica could see three men sitting at a desk, one of them angrily thumping the desktop with one stubby finger. The clerk bent over and said something into this man's ear.

"Christ!" she heard him say. Rising, he chased the others from his office and stood in the doorway, thumbs hooked into his vest pockets, studying Jessie.

"Mr. Strangfeld?"

"You must be her," the man said instead of answering. "I heard the big boss was the most beautiful woman this side of New York. Come in, come in."

Strangfeld was thickly built. His eyes were dark,

pouched, his jowls beginning to sag. He had the hands of a working man and wore his suit and tie as if he was uncomfortable in them and would as soon exchange them for bib overalls. Jessie could read nothing at all in his expression or his lifeless eyes.

He sat at his desk, leaned far back in his chair, and lit a nasty-smelling cigar. After a minute spent just staring at her he leaned forward.

"When I asked for help in this, I didn't think Pearson would go all the way up the line."

"Abel Pearson didn't notify me," Jessica answered.

"Who did?"

"No one. Believe it or not, this is quite coincidental. I came to Beaverton on another matter entirely."

"Hard to swallow."

"I just told you it was so," Jessica said stiffly. "The man Pearson sent has arrived, however; his name is Dancer. If he hasn't been here already, he soon will be."

Strangfeld nodded almost disinterestedly. "All right."

"You know the marshal is of the opinion that someone on the inside must be tipping off the thieves."

"I've heard King's theory before, yeah," Strangfeld said sourly, stubbing out his cigar.

"You don't give it any credence?"

Strangfeld shrugged. "Maybe. I've made every effort to keep the date and route of our shipments secret. You should inquire at the freight office."

"I have," Jessica answered. "I happen to know Earl Gibbons and I don't believe he has any knowledge of how the information is getting out."

"You believe I do?" Strangfeld asked, crossing his forearms as he leaned across the desk.

"I have no idea. I hope not."

Strangfeld looked toward the corner hatrack. He lifted his chin slightly in that direction. "If you want me to resign, lady, I'll get my hat and walk out of here right now. I been doing my best to run this operation, and believe me, it hasn't been easy. If you're calling me a crook, I'll go."

"No one called you a crook," Jessica said. She paused,

letting Strangfeld relax a little before she went on. "I understand you've had trouble with some of your laborers."

"The Japanese."

"That's what they tell me."

"I've had some, sure," Strangfeld said, looking defensive for the first time. "Nothing serious."

"What sort of trouble?" Jessica inquired. Strangfeld shifted uneasily in his chair.

"Some of 'em don't speak the language very well."

"And?"

"Some of 'em don't think they're being paid enough, I guess," Strangfeld said. "And they got the idea that they get the dirty jobs—mucking out the stopes and such."

"Is it true?"

"Someone's got to do it, don't they?" Strangfeld asked in exasperation.

"Yes," Jessica agreed. "Someone has to. I'll want to take a look at your books before I leave."

"What for?"

"To see just how much the Japanese are getting paid," Jessica answered. Strangfeld heaved a frustrated sigh.

"It's less. I told you. Listen, one reason for hiring these immigrants is because they'll work for less. I'm trying to save the company money."

"Save it somewhere else," Jessie responded.

"Not that it matters a hell of a lot," Strangfeld said in a quieter voice. "The way things are going, Centennial will be busted in three months."

"No it won't," Jessie promised. "How's the ore holding up?"

"Rich, still." Strangfeld got to his feet. "As a matter of fact, we're going up a new vein that looks real promising."

"I'll want to see that as well," Jessica told the startled mine manager.

"You don't mean you want to go down in the mine?"

"Of course."

"It's dangerous down there, for a woman."

"For anyone. There are Japanese women working down there, aren't there?"

"Yeah, but . . ." Strangfeld gave it up. He wasn't going to win an argument with this hellcat. Anyone who knew Jessica Starbuck could have told him that.

Jessica looked over the payroll records in the outer office and told Strangfeld, "We won't have this anymore. Understand? Everyone gets the same pay for the same work."

"Yes, Miss Starbuck," Strangfeld answered. "It's your money, isn't it?"

"Yes," Jessie replied, "it is."

Outside, it was cold and cloudy with a north wind blowing. Strangfeld, in his overcoat now, walked with her toward the head of the shaft.

"When is the next shipment of silver going out?" Jessica asked.

Strangfeld gave her a sideways glance and hesitated for a moment before answering. "Thursday," he said, nearly under his breath.

"Does the marshal know? Gibbons?"

"No one knows yet. I'll let them know the day before."

"You're being pretty cautious."

"Shouldn't I be?" Strangfeld answered. "We've lost something in the neighborhood of eighty thousand dollars over the last two months."

The mine was in full swing when Jessica entered it and borrowed a steel miner's hat to wear down. She noticed the timbering, decided it was done properly, and followed Strangfeld down, riding in an ore cart which ran along rusted steel rails.

Japanese and American miners worked steadily on either side of the main shaft. Women with rags around their heads pushed huge wheelbarrows loaded with ore to the mule-drawn carts.

The new vein looked promising; it was two feet wide now, and appeared to be widening as the miners followed it deeper into the heart of the mountain.

Outside again, Strangfeld asked, "Well?"

"It looks all right. Where's the smelter?"

"Downslope, around the bend there. You want to see that too, I expect."

Jessica just smiled in answer. When the next lumbering ore wagon came past, guarded by a man with a rifle, Jessie and Strangfeld hopped up onto the tailgate and rode along toward the smelter.

Two men with Winchesters stood outside the main entrance to the faded green building. Inside, Strangfeld greeted a man at the desk and led Jessica through to where the ore was being melted down and refined. Beyond that huge room, where the great caldrons filled with molten silver were being skimmed for impurities, was the storeroom.

Again there were armed men. Strangfeld produced a key and led Jessica into a windowless room where bars of refined silver sat stacked neatly on pallets. Jessica picked one up, hefted it, and put it down again.

"You've seen about everything there is to see," Strangfeld said. "And I've got work to do."

"All right," she answered. "I may be back, though."

"Anytime," Strangfeld said with some irony. "You're the boss." He had another thought. "What about when this detective or whatever he is that Pearson sent down comes around?"

"Give him the tour too," Jessica said after a minute's thought.

"All right. Want me to tell him when the shipment's leaving?"

Briefly Jessica pictured the lean blue-eyed man with the infuriating smile she had met at Gibbons's office. "No," she said finally, "don't tell Dancer that. The fewer that know, the better."

There was some sort of commotion near the mine office when Jessica and Strangfeld reached it again. Four or five men were gathered around the bed of a wagon. One of them gestured wildly toward Strangfeld, who glanced at Jessie and picked up his pace.

There was a dead man in the back of the wagon.

"Found him up the road, Mr. Strangfeld. Not dead long."

"Do you know him?" Jessica asked.

"Hell, yes, I know him. Lou Seivers. He's one of my guards." Strangfeld removed his hat and wiped back his hair. "Damn it all, who could've done it?"

That question Jessica knew the answer to. She had done it herself. The bearded man in the back of the wagon was one of those who had attacked her on the trail.

It meant something, but exactly what, Jessica wasn't sure. Strangfeld looked genuinely surprised and upset, but then he might have just been upset that his men had blown the job of killing Jessica Starbuck before she could start poking around the operation.

Maybe.

"What's wrong?" a man on horseback asked. Jessie turned to find Michael Dancer, hat tugged low, watching her. He could see very well what was wrong, so Jessica didn't bother to answer him.

"I've told Mr. Strangfeld to show you around," she said instead.

"Yes?" Dancer's eyes narrowed and twinkled as he leaned forward, arms resting on the saddlehorn. "I was hoping you might do that yourself, Miss Starbuck."

"And hinder your investigation? I wouldn't think of it."

Dancer grinned. "There is one thing I wanted to check with you," he said, and nodded his head away from the wagon and knot of men there. Jessica followed him to the shade of a huge oak tree and watched as Dancer swung down.

"What is it?" she asked.

"True the silver shipment's going out Thursday?" Dancer asked, wiping out his hat band. Jessica just stared at him for a long while.

"How could you know that? No one's supposed to."

27

"It is Thursday then. Thanks," he said, putting his hat back in place as his grin deepened. Jessica felt herself growing furious. She knew it showed on her face, yet there was nothing she could do about it. The tall investigator had the power to fluster her like few men had ever had.

"How?" Jessica repeated.

"Nothing to it. Centennial hires its animals—mules and horses. I stopped by the local stable. Strangfeld wants ten fresh mules Thursday morning. That's not a regular thing."

Jessica muttered under her breath. What she said wasn't real ladylike, and Dancer grinned again. "Yeah," he agreed.

"I wonder how many other holes there are in Strangfeld's security. Put him wise to this one, will you, Dancer? Tell him I've authorized him to purchase his animals and to stop hiring them. I suppose he was trying to save money by hiring mules. It might have been a very expensive idea."

"I'll tell him . . . Oh," Dancer said, halting and turning back, "I think we'd better have dinner tonight, talk things over, don't you?"

"Is there something else to talk about?" Jessica asked.

"There might be. You have to eat anyway, don't you? Why don't I pick you up around seven?"

"Mr. Dancer, I don't think I even like you."

He grinned again, swinging onto his horse's back. "That's all right, Miss Starbuck. You will. You will."

Then he wheeled his horse and walked it slowly across the yard toward the mine office, whistling as he went. Jessie stood staring at his broad back for a minute before she realized she too was smiling. Then she shook her head and started back toward town. It was a long walk and it was brisk, but it would do her good, she decided; it might help clear her head—about a number of things

Ki had the feeling he was simply wasting a day.

He walked through the narrow alleys of the Japanese shanty town, smelling the rice cooking, the occasional scent of incense. Religious banners fluttered in the wind. Here and there, kids, bundled to their ears, stared with wide, dark eyes at the tall man.

He had already asked at the few local businesses, a small laundry, an almost hidden restaurant where a lone man was preparing *sushi,* a knife-sharpening establishment. No one knew of a girl named Yoshiko.

Ki pondered that fact. Even if it wasn't his Yoshiko, there had been a woman of that name here. She had made her presence well enough known. The Japanese were simply not talking about it.

Passing an open door he glanced into a shack and saw an old woman in black sitting crosslegged on her mat, brewing tea. She looked up, grinned toothlessly, and gestured for Ki to enter her home.

Ducking low, Ki walked to her, bowed, and at her invitation seated himself across the mat from her.

"You will have tea?" she asked in Japanese.

"Yes, that would be very good. It's a long time since I had real tea," Ki answered.

"So you are Japanese. I thought so, but there is something . . ."

"I am part American," Ki answered, taking the tea.

"Oh, part American, yes," the old woman replied, chuckling to herself. She apparently found this interesting and amusing. Ki lifted his tiny cup of tea to his lips and sipped at it.

"It is very good. Thank you."

"I saw you go by before. I saw you go by and then come back the other way. Are you lost?"

"I was looking for someone," Ki said, putting his cup down.

"Yes? Someone I know?" the old woman asked.

"Perhaps. A girl named Yoshiko."

"Yoshiko?" The old woman's face clouded and then cleared. She lifted one finger into the air. "Ah! I know Yoshiko. She used to help me clean up my poor house. She is gone now." The smile vanished and she shook her head worriedly.

"How long ago was it that you saw her?" Ki asked, trying to keep the excitement out of his voice.

"Yoshiko? Not long. A little while. Maybe a few weeks..."

Behind Ki someone entered the house. He turned his head to see a young Japanese man with broad shoulders glaring at him. "Mother, don't be a fool! Why are you talking to this man? Don't you know what he is?"

The old woman was thrown into utter confusion. She actually drew away from Ki, studying him as if she had brought a wolf into her house. "I don't understand," she said weakly.

Her son ignored her. "You," he said, leveling a finger at Ki. "Get out of my house. Now."

"What have I done to offend you?" Ki asked mildly.

"Go!" The finger was trembling now. Fear was etched into the young man's face. "Now, before it is too late."

Ki glanced again at the old woman, shrugged, and got to his feet. There was no point in arguing, if the man wanted him to leave. "I wish you would explain your anger," Ki said. He took a step toward the young man, hands spread. The man nearly fell down trying to back away.

It was no use. Ki looked at the old woman and her trembling son, nodded, and ducked out of the house into the sunlight.

The alleyway was no longer deserted. Five young Japanese, scarfs around their heads, were waiting, watching him with barely concealed malice. Ki nodded to them and turned away, striding up the alley.

They followed him at a distance, silently. One of them had produced a hatchet from his belt and was swinging it in his right hand. They meant business.

Ki turned into another, smaller alley and wound his way among the shanties. The footsteps were nearer now. The *te* master stopped and turned to face them.

"What do you want?" he asked them quietly. When there was no answer, he repeated the question in Japanese.

It was their leader, the one with the hatchet who answered. "Your blood," he said, just before he leaped at Ki. His razor-edged weapon sliced through the air toward Ki's skull.

Chapter 4

Ki shifted his feet only slightly, crossed his arms at the wrists, and blocked the downward arc of the hatchet. His powerful hands gripped the attacker's forearm, and the man, minus his hatchet, found himself flying through the air to land on his face against the gravel of the alleyway, losing a few teeth in the process.

The second thug was right on the heels of the first. Whatever ideas he might have had were knocked out of his head as Ki sidekicked him, his heel landing flush on the man's nose, sending him reeling back against the wall of a shack to sag to the ground, his nose streaming blood.

The remaining three formed a loose half-circle around Ki and moved in more cautiously. Ki's hand dipped inside one of the inner pockets of his leather vest and emerged with three *shuriken*, deadly throwing stars. Sunlight winked on the *te* master's weapons, and the thugs changed their minds in a hurry.

With a yell, they took to their heels, leaving two of their number behind. Ki tucked the *shuriken* away and walked to the leader, the one who lay sprawled on his face. Yanking up both of the man's sleeves, Ki found the tiger tattoos on his forearms. With disgust Ki let the man slide to the ground again.

The other one had the same marks on his arms, and Ki shook his head. Things didn't get any simpler, only more complex. He had found no trace of Yoshiko, but he had found a different sort of trouble, one inexplicable to him.

It was getting late and he had no wish to stay in the

shantytown any longer anyway, and so he started back toward the hotel, passing homeward-bound Japanese miners.

At the hotel he knocked on Jessica's door and went in to sit on her bed as she brushed out her long, honey blond hair in front of the mirror. She had shed her jeans and shirt and was now wearing a blue dress Ki had never seen before, apparently purchased in town.

"You have an appointment?" Ki asked.

"Maybe."

She turned, showing off the dress which clung to her breasts intriguingly and followed the long tapering lines of her thighs. "Someone I know?" Ki asked.

"Not yet."

"He is a lucky man," Ki decided. Although he didn't feel romantically inclined toward Jessica Starbuck, he would have had to be a blind man not to notice how beautiful she was and how other men looked at her. There was hunger in their eyes as Jessica passed them on the street, an understandable hunger.

"You assume it's a man," Jessica said with a smile.

"I know it is from the way you look," Ki answered.

She sat next to him on the bed and took his callused hand. "A man called Michael Dancer, Ki. He's been sent down here by Pearson to look into the robberies. He's far from stupid. He put something together today as a matter of fact, something that hadn't occurred to me." She told him about Centennial's policy of hiring fresh animals for the long haul to the capital.

"Yes. So simple, but easy to overlook. You put a stop to that, I take it."

"Yes, I did." She stood and went to the window to look out at the sundown sky above the mountain peaks. "Did I tell you I had to kill a man today?"

"You know you didn't," Ki answered with concern.

"An ambush attempt. One of the men was a guard at Centennial."

"You are certain?"

"Strangfeld identified him."

"Strangfeld," Ki said meditatively. "And what sort of man is he?"

"I'm not sure. Bull-headed. He has been giving the Japanese the dirty work at the mine and paying them half as much as anyone else."

Ki just nodded. He didn't have to ask Jessica if she had done something about that. Her father had instilled a strong sense of right and wrong in the woman.

"Things may be easier now," Ki said, only half believing it. "The Japanese were bound to hold a grudge against a mine owner who was cheating them."

"Did you run into a lot of resentment?" Jessie asked.

"Resentment," Ki repeated. No, it wasn't resentment he had encountered, but something more than that. It was hatred, fear. He told Jessica that and then told her about the attack by the young men in the alley.

"Why you? Why attack you, Ki? Were they just local toughs who wanted to rob you, do you think?"

"No. They asked for nothing. They only wanted to kill me. I'm sure they knew who I was. They were gangsters, Jessica. If they were Chinese, you would say Tong members. This particular gang is called *Sendai*. They are numerous in Japan in the large cities."

"You're sure?"

"They wore the markings of the gang. A tiger tattooed so, on both forearms."

"Does this have something to do with Yoshiko, Ki?" Jessica asked. Ki could only shrug.

"I do not know now what anything has to do with anything. The mine, the attack at Gibbons's office, these thugs today, the men who tried to kill you, Yoshiko. I do not mind puzzles, Jessica, but this one has no starting place."

But it did to Jessica's mind. It had been the start of everything. *Yoshiko*. "There is no trace of her?"

"No, but they know, Jessica, they know."

There was a rap at the door, and as it swung open they turned to see Michael Dancer in a dark suit and hat standing there. He glanced at Ki and then grinned at Jessica.

"Ready?" His eyes combed her carefully.

"Almost. This is Ki, my very good friend. Ki, Michael Dancer." The two men shook hands. "Give Ki time to change and we'll be off," Jessica said. Some disappointment showed in Dancer's eyes, but he nodded amiably enough.

By the time Ki had changed into his blue suit and rinsed off, Dancer had managed to get close enough to Jessica to slip his arm around her small waist as they stood at the window watching the last dying flames of sunset. She didn't pull away or act coy; rather, she had leaned her head against his shoulder. Dancer was glowing with pleasure.

"I am ready," Ki said from the doorway.

"Great," Dancer said with limited enthusiasm. He looked Ki up and down and added, "The way things have been going, maybe you don't want to go out unarmed."

"I am armed," Ki said and Dancer's eyes narrowed. He shrugged, picked up Jessica's white shawl, and put his hat on.

"All right then. Let's see how much damage the restaurant can do to a steak."

Very little damage, as it turned out. The meat was juicy and pink inside. Jessica dug into it eagerly. Ki only chewed on a roll and drank the weak tea he had been served. When Dancer was finished he leaned back in his chair contentedly. Without making a show of it he looked around the tiny restaurant and then said quietly, "All right. What do we do about Thursday?"

"We?" Jessica said. "You're assuming a lot all of a sudden, aren't you, Michael?"

Dancer shrugged. "I'm assuming we both want to accomplish the same thing. It's your mine; you don't want to see it go bust. With me—well, it's my job, isn't it? I was sent here to stop this highway robbery." He paused. "Unless you don't trust me, Miss Starbuck."

She looked steadily at Dancer. This was a decision she had to make then and there. Why not trust Dancer? He obviously hadn't been around to take part in the raids. Besides, Pearson trusted him.

"All right. What do *we* do about it?"

35

Dancer smiled. "The obvious thing to do is stop the shipment. Scratch Thursday and find a new day. If the leak was going through the stable, then it's been closed now."

"And if it wasn't?" Jessica said. "If the leak is through Gibbons's freight office or out of the mine, then our new date will be no better than the last and Centennial will have missed another delivery and probably its payroll."

Ki nodded his agreement. "The shipment must be made Thursday."

Dancer argued, "The wagons will just be hit again, no matter how many extra guards we put on."

"I did not intend to put more guards on," Ki replied. This time Jessie was the one to give him a puzzled glance.

"But Ki," she said, "what else is there to do? I was planning on doubling our guards."

"Then perhaps the outlaws will double their forces. Then perhaps twice as many men will get hurt or killed. No, that is not the way to handle this."

"You have a better idea?" Dancer asked.

"I think so, yes. We will have to talk to Strangfeld about it. He won't like what I have to suggest, but it will work; I know it. Tell me, Dancer," Ki said, leaning across the table, hands clasped. "It is correct that the outlaws never take the wagons, isn't it?"

"How could they? There's nowhere to run with a wagonload of silver. The roads go only from here to the capital. No, they grab what they can and jam it into their saddlebags or burlap sacks."

"Yes," Ki said almost to himself. "Then it will work."

"Are you going to let us in on it or not, Ki?" Jessica asked. He told them. Dancer just sat there staring in amazement at Ki. Jessica was grinning broadly.

"Maybe," she said. "Just maybe. Do you think there's time to do it, Ki?"

"It seems to me there would be. Strangfeld will know. We will talk to him tomorrow."

"Someone," Dancer said, "is going to get a hell of a surprise. I hope you're right about this, Ki. It could solve everything."

No, not everything. There were too many other things going on. But, Ki hoped, he had the solution to getting at least one load of silver through.

Outside, it was cool and clouding up again. Jessica and Dancer turned toward the hotel as Ki stood breathing in deeply. He felt like another walk, perhaps down toward the Japanese side of town again. It was dangerous, yes, but where else could he hope to fine out about Yoshiko?

Stepping off the boardwalk he passed two ladies and nodded to them, his head moving three inches. It was then that he heard death, heard it whisper in his ear, a humming promise of a violent end.

The women walked on, hearing nothing, seeing nothing. Ki crouched, watching the alley across the street. He started that way, had his path blocked by a freight wagon and then a man on horseback. By the time he got to the alley there was no one there.

Ki recrossed the street and searched the walls of the restaurant, finding nothing. It was in one of the awning's pole uprights that he found what he was looking for. It sent a shiver up Ki's spine.

The *shuriken* was deep red with a blue diamond marked on it. Ki yanked it from the pole, knowing that it was indeed death he had heard whisper to him. He was alive just then only because he had been gentleman enough to bow his head toward two ladies, shifting his skull forward a bare few inches.

He and Jessica had had problems before, but this was different. It was more deadly, more sure, than anything they had encountered yet in Beaverton.

Ki realized in the back of his mind that he had feared this all along. Tiny subconscious warnings had been sounding in the back of his mind for days, but he had refused to pay attention to them. Now there was no choice. Death was here. It was out there in the darkness now, stalking Ki in a very personal way.

He weighed the strange *shuriken* in his hand and then tucked it away.

For a long while Ki stood staring at the night as people

brushed past him. Finally he turned away, whispering, "I know you are here, Kobi-san. I know you are here, waiting."

Jessica Starbuck struck a match to light the lamp on her hotel-room vanity, and Dancer put his hand over hers. "You really need to light that now?" he asked.

She turned slowly toward him, the match still burning between her fingers as Dancer's arms went around her, drawing her to meet his urgent kiss.

She didn't resist it. Her lips parted and her body pressed against his, fitting itself to his contours. Her breasts, flattened against his chest, rose and fell in little fluttering motions.

The match fell from Jessica's fingers. "You take a lot for granted," she said.

"Do I?" He kissed her again, even harder, his hands reaching down to clench her buttocks and pull her to him. Jessica could feel the rising need of his body against her pelvis.

"Let go," she said and her voice was whispery.

"If I have to," Dancer said, kissing her once more, lightly before his hands fell away and Jessica stepped back. In the darkness, he heard the whisper of fabric against skin, and when she stepped back into his arms his hands found cool, naked flesh.

Dancer swept her from the floor and carried her to the bed. Then he undressed as Jessica arranged the pillows. He was in bed beside her in half a minute, his hard body against the yielding flesh of her softly curved body.

His hands roamed her breasts and thighs as his lips touched her throat, ears, and shoulders gently before returning to her parted lips. Jessie make a small contented sound, looped her arms around his neck, and shifted her legs so that Dancer slid naturally between them.

Her hands roamed his buttocks, drawing him a little nearer with each nudging motion. She could feel him poised and ready, heard his accelerated breathing in her ear.

"You take a whole lot for granted." She laughed as her hand dipped between his thighs and found his swollen shaft. She positioned him deftly, and with a gentle thrust of her hips, took him inside. Dancer's entire body went rigid and he gripped her shoulders hard enough to bruise them. Jessica arched her back and took him into the hilt.

For a moment she lay still, enjoying the sensation as her fingers traced the knuckled line of his spine. Dancer held back for as long as possible, but then he began a gentle swaying which became a driving, needful assault.

Jessica's legs lifted and wrapped around Dancer's waist as he moved against her, his powerful body having but a single purpose now. Jessica clung to him, her knees lifting even higher. She gripped her ankles and held her smooth white legs out like magnificent wings, giving Dancer full access to her body.

Through half-closed eyes Jessica could see the intent face of the man on top of her, and she felt the buzzing in her head become a tingling which rushed across her body from nipples to groin. The rush of fluid which followed surprised her; it came so quickly. She trembled and clung even more tightly to Dancer, knowing that her own sudden dampness had lifted him to an even higher level of intensity.

He was rough, solid, and strong, driving against Jessica time and again. Each thrust turned on lights in Jessica's skull. She felt herself rising to a new peak, felt her body tremble, heard a moan escape from her lips as Dancer, rigid now from head to toes, drove it home one last time and found his own deep climax.

They lay together, Dancer still working against her, more gently now, swaying from side to side as Jessie, depleted, rubbed his back and shoulders with gentle fingers.

"Bastard," she whispered playfully. "That was too fast."

Dancer propped himself up on one elbow. "Was it?" He kissed her lips and smiled. "How can I make up for it?"

"Do it again," Jessica whispered. And he did.

* * *

Morning was cool. Sunlight winked through the old lace curtains on the hotel room window. Dancer was gone. Jessica rolled over, hugging the pillow for a while before she rose from the tangled bed and dressed in jeans and flannel shirt, buckling on the peachwood-handled, slate-gray .38 revolver.

She brushed her hair vigorously, put on her flat crowned hat, and went out down the hall to Ki's room.

He was up and dressed, his door standing open. He turned at her approach and said, "The Centennial?"

"After breakfast."

"Strangfeld isn't going to like this much."

Jessica smiled. "It really doesn't matter what he likes, Ki." And then her eyes fell on the *shuriken* on Ki's dresser. She frowned and walked closer, fingered the unfamiliar throwing star, studying its markings. "This isn't yours, Ki."

"No, it isn't."

"Then . . .?"

"Someone tried to kill me with it last night." He shrugged.

Jessica's forehead furrowed. "You know who it was."

"Yes, I know. Kobi-san."

"Kobi-san?" Jessica searched her memory briefly. "Yoshiko's grandfather. Your Master."

"Yes, the Master."

"I don't understand, Ki—what does this mean?"

"He wishes to kill me, that is all. Unless I can speak to him I cannot understand why. It too has something to do with Yoshiko; it must. Kobi-san and I parted as friends, as master and pupil."

"How could he be here in Beaverton? And why, Ki? He must be old by now, very old."

"Old, yes," Ki answered. He added ironically, "But obviously still skilled at his craft. Only chance saved my life last night, not an errant eye or unsure hand."

Ki could say nothing more to satisfy Jessica's curiosity.

They had walked into a situation which continued to snarl upon itself, forming loop after loop of mystery.

"Have you seen Dancer?" Ki asked.

"Not this morning."

Ki didn't look happy. "I hope we're not making a mistake with him."

"Ki! Don't be so suspicious. It's obvious that Dancer couldn't have been here when the robberies were pulled. Strangfeld just sent for him. He's only been in town a day or two. Pearson wouldn't send anyone he wasn't sure of."

"No, you are right," Ki answered, his voice flat.

"What's the matter, Ki?" Jessica asked, turning him by his arm. "We know who he is."

"Yes. Perhaps." Ki shrugged with one shoulder. "If he *is* Michael Dancer. It he *is* the man Pearson sent. I am not saying he isn't, but we know none of that. I would suggest a wire to Pearson."

"You're being overly cautious now, aren't you?"

"Perhaps. But we have invited Dancer into our small circle. He will know everything we have planned. A little caution can't hurt, Jessica."

"If it makes you happy," Jessie sighed. "I'll wire after breakfast."

"Jessica—ask for a description too, will you?"

Jessie looked at Ki and nodded almost imperceptibly. Ki was right, of course, but it seemed he was looking for things to worry about—as if they didn't already have enough.

By the time they had finished breakfast there was still no sign of Dancer. Jessica sent the wire to Pearson asking for an immediate reply, and they set out for Centennial, ready to face an unhappy Strangfeld.

Unhappy wasn't the word. He was irate. In a fury he shook his finger at both of them, his jaw trembling. "Do you know how much work this is going to be? This mad plan of yours?"

"Yes. I want it done, though. If your people have to work around the clock, I want it done."

"Miss Starbuck . . ." Strangfeld sagged into his chair,

spreading his hands in a plea. "I've tried to cooperate. But you've marched in here wanting to reorganize everything from our pay scale to the way we hire livestock. Now this. Lady, you are a terror."

"And the owner."

"I offered my resignation before," Strangfeld said stiffly. "You can still have it."

"I don't want it, Mr. Strangfeld. I simply want you to do this my way. I know how and why you did things in the past—and you know that your way hasn't been working worth a damn."

Strangfeld didn't answer; he was so furious, he couldn't. He just nodded, forming his big hands into tight knots.

"The men who are assigned to this job must not be allowed to leave the premises before the Thursday shipment has gone out," Ki said. Strangfeld glanced acidly at this new interloper.

"They'll want to go home—to eat, to be with their families," the mine manager said slowly, trying to contain his temper.

"There will be a bonus in this for them," Jessica said. "A substantial bonus, enough to soothe any hard feelings. Ki is right. No one who works on this can leave the grounds."

Strangfeld closed his eyes and lowered his head. They could almost read his thoughts. Why had this woman drifted in from nowhere to plague him? He rose abruptly and walked to the door connecting the inner and outer offices.

"Shore! Get over to the smelter and have them fire it up."

"Now?"

"Do it, dammit! I'll be along in a while to explain things." He banged the door shut and turned sharply toward Jessica Starbuck. "Satisfied?" he demanded.

"Yes. Now I'm satisfied."

Jessica and Ki rode back toward town through a drizzling rain which veiled the mountains and chilled their flesh. The wire was waiting for them at the hotel.

Jessica read it once and read it again. "It's from Pearson—'Sent investigator on nineteenth. Good man. Former federal marshal named Jack Troupe. Pearson.'"

Chapter 5

The meeting was held Thursday morning before the sun had crept over the eastern horizon. Jessica and Ki were there, Earl Gibbons and Jack Taylor, Marshal King, and the teamsters who would be making the run to the capital with the silver from Centennial.

Jessica was listening as Ki explained what was going on, but only with a part of her mind.

Michael Dancer was an impostor. Pearson had sent a man down, all right, but a man named Troupe. Troupe hadn't arrived, but Dancer, claiming to be the investigator, had. She had been wrong about men before, but this one hurt. Dancer had seemed like the real thing.

The marshal, one leg propped up on a crate, listened to Ki's plan carefully, but without showing much enthusiasm. Technically, as town marshal he had nothing to do with events outside the town limits, but being the only law within a hundred miles made it advisable for him to know what was happening.

Gibbons, leaner now, and still bandaged, was enthused. He kept slapping his knee and saying, "This'll teach 'em."

Jack Taylor and the teamsters weren't so sure. "This might get 'em mad enough to gun us all down," Taylor commented sourly.

"Hell, they're liable to do that anyway, anytime they take a notion," Gibbons answered.

"That's the plan," Ki said quietly. "If anyone wants out, it's all right. I'll drive a wagon myself."

Taylor growled, "That's not what I meant. We've driven

past these bastards before, been shot at and held up and threatened. I reckon we can do it again."

"Then it's settled," Ki said.

"It's settled."

"Marshal?" Ki asked, "Anything to say?"

"Yeah." King turned his head and spat as he rose. "Good luck."

That they would need. Outside, the teamsters were hitching Centennial's newly purchased mules to their freight wagons. On each bench seat a man with a shotgun watched. At the mine Strangfeld's people would be carting the bullion from the safe room to the outer doors. There too men with guns would be watching for anything unusual. But the outlaws wouldn't strike yet; they had always waited until the wagons were out on the open plains. This time should be no different.

King nodded, spat again and sauntered off to make his rounds, looking like a man who wasn't entirely convinced. With Gibbons on his feet again, Jack Taylor had returned to his driving duties. He pulled on his gauntlets, ran a hand over the flank of one of the mules, and clambered aboard.

Jessica asked Gibbons, "Why don't you use your own stock, Earl?"

"It's in the contract," Gibbons said dryly. "We lost too many good mules trying to haul that silver down-country. One of their tricks is to drop a few mules to halt the wagons. It got damned expensive. Now Centennial provides the animals."

Jessica still wasn't paying complete attention. A tall man on a strapping palomino rode past and she lifted her eyes. No, it wasn't Dancer—and just where had he vanished to?

Ki was walking to his own horse when he heard the whisper from the alley. He stopped, shifting his balance just in case, but it was only a small Japanese boy, beckoning with one finger.

Ki walked that way, his eyes searching the alley behind the boy. "What is it?" Ki asked.

"Yoshiko?"

45

"What did you say?" Without meaning to, Ki gripped his arm so tightly that the boy winced.

"Yoshiko?" the boy repeated, his eyes widening. Ki loosened his grip and bent low, looking intently into the boy's eyes.

"What about her? Where is she?"

The boy was frightened and for a minute Ki thought he wasn't going to answer. "Here," he said finally, and he pressed a folded piece of paper into Ki's palm before he turned and raced away up the alley.

Ki opened the note and read the two words there: "Castle Walls." They meant nothing at all to him, and he raised his eyes again, but the boy was gone. Castle Walls. What in hell could that mean? Jessica was calling to him and Ki stuffed the note into his vest pocket, turning back toward the street to lead his horse and Jessica's toward the waiting wagons.

"What is it, Ki?" she asked, reading the puzzlement on Ki's face.

"Nothing." There was no point in going into it now, and no time. Jack Taylor popped his long-handled whip over the ears of the mule team, and the wagon creaked forward, moving off along the road toward Centennial mine.

Ki rode silently beside Jessica Starbuck. The wind was rising and the sun climbed higher into the sky, splashing the horizontal clouds with color. The pines swayed in the wind. The wagons creaked along with only the occasional shout of a teamster or the loud crack of a whip breaking the silence.

Strangfeld, looking no happier than ever, was waiting at the gate to the mine. He stepped onto one of the wagons, giving Jessie and Ki a single scathing glance. He looked weary and rumpled. He had undoubtedly spent the last twenty-four hours sitting up, urging his men on.

Castle Walls. Ki pondered it one more time and then pushed thoughts of Yoshiko and the enigmatic message aside. There was another job to be done now. Once the silver was loaded they were fair game for the outlaws— and they knew the bullion was coming.

Beyond the hills surrounding Beaverton and the mine, the land flattened to a series of rolling hills with only occasional timber. The road the wagons followed stretched out in a nearly straight line toward the south. Beside them four outriders rode, armed and wary.

To the west two more riders followed the progress of the wagons from a distance. Jessica Starbuck rode a paint pony and the *te* master, Ki, was astride a loose-gaited sorrel gelding.

Their eyes were on the wagons, on the country around, searching for natural ambush points, but each of them rode with other thoughts. Dancer. Castle Walls.

The fake investigator crowded against Jessie's thoughts as Yoshiko nagged Ki's concentration on the job at hand. They glanced at each other as their horses wove their way through the cedar and pine woods, but neither of them spoke just then.

They were ahead of the wagons now. The trail passed beneath the foot of a butte, where they drew their horses up. Opposite them was another butte, crumbling, cedar-stippled.

"What do we do, Ki, if they hit the wagons?"

"Nothing, unless it is necessary to save a life. They mustn't know we are here. I intend to follow them home this time."

Ki was right, Jessica knew. Shooting a few of the outlaws wasn't going to help anything. The country was full of fresh recruits. What was needed was to find the head of the gang and cut it off. Find their leader.

Jessie had puzzled over that one—just who was running this gang? She had suspected Strangfeld, but now was not sure. Dancer was another possibility—one she refused to dwell on. Who else? Jack Taylor? Earl Gibbons himself?—although Jessica found that solution improbable. Someone they had never met or imagined, then.

Except the gang had always had inside information, had always known which wagon trains were decoys, what day the silver would actually leave Centennial. No, it had to be someone in Beaverton, someone connected with the operation . . .

"Look." Jessica nudged Ki, but he only nodded; he had already seen them.

Seven mounted men sat the rim of the butte opposite. They wore bandannas over their faces and held their rifles ready. Ki's eyes scanned the land below, and finally he picked out the second group of men in a dry gully south of the road. Four, he counted, but there may have been more hidden there.

Ki, feeling himself tense, glanced at Jessica, who had closed her hand around the butt of her pistol. He shook his head. They had to go through with the plan. He only hoped the outriders and shotgun guards had taken heed of his instructions to surrender immediately and not make a fight of it.

Jessica felt her chest tighten as the riders lifted their mounts up out of the gully. Opposite her, the rest of the outlaws had started slowly forward. At a signal from their leader they charged down the slope as gunfire began from near the gully. One outrider went down, clutching his leg, and Jessica reflexively unsheathed her Winchester.

Ki's eyes were fixed on the short, furious exchange of fire. One outlaw hit the ground, rolled and lay unmoving against the dusty ground. A dozen more shots were fired, but the outriding guards were trapped and outnumbered. They simply gave it up as the teamsters halted their wagons.

Jack Taylor saw Pat Julian go down holding his leg, and he cursed savagely, drawing his revolver but not firing it. Pat was a good friend, and he had three kids at home.

Taylor followed orders. He dropped his pistol to the floor of the wagon box and halted the mule team. The outlaws surrounded the wagons, waving rifles. One of them vaulted from his horse to the bed of the wagon.

"Where is it?" he demanded, sticking the muzzle of a .44 Colt in Taylor's face.

"You're standing on it, you fool," Taylor spat back. He was too mad to use discretion.

"Throw back the tarp," another outlaw shouted, and the one in the back did so. He stared down and then looked up in dismay, a curse frothing from his lips.

"What is it? Dammit, start handing the bars over! We can't sit here all day."

"Ain't bars," the man in the wagonbed said.

"What?" The other rider shifted his horse, looked into the wagonbed himself, and breathed out an equally profane curse. He turned on Jack Taylor with a snarl. "What's this?"

"Looks like silver to me," Taylor said.

"You know what I mean!"

"That's the way they wanted it shipped. Me, I just haul it, Mister," Taylor answered.

"Some smart-ass bastard . . ." the outlaw muttered.

"What's holding us up, Earl?" another raider asked. The gun he held on an outrider was beginning to waver a little. He was obviously nervous. "Start passing out the bars."

"Bars! Take a look, you son of a bitch. They cut a new mold and cast the shit into cannonballs. Cannonballs, but they've got to weigh a hundred and fifty pounds each. Take a look!" He ripped the tarp back the rest of the way. "Try tucking those away in your saddlebags—if you can even pick one up!"

Ki couldn't hear the voices at this distance, but he knew that at least a part of his plan had worked. He had told Strangfeld to recast the silver into the ungainly hundred-and-seventy-pound balls—no problem for the freight wagons to carry, but impossible for the horse-mounted thieves to carry off.

There was another heated argument below, and some gun-waving, but no shots were fired. The outlaws simply pulled out in frustration in the end.

When they were gone, their dust streaking the sky, Ki started toward the wagons. Jessica, riding beside him, touched his arm.

"Ki, aren't we going to follow them?"

He looked to the plume of dust. "We will catch up. I want to see one thing."

49

What he wanted to see was the dead outlaw. Ki swung down from his horse, yanked the mask down, revealing a distinctly oriental face, and then rolled up the dead man's sleeve to reveal the tiger tattoo. Ki crouched there for a minute, staring at the outlaw unhappily.

Jack Taylor and two other men were at his shoulder now, and one of them muttered, "A damn Jap! It's the damn Japs behind this."

That was all they needed. Ki rose and dusted off his hands. As he turned toward his horse the angry eyes of the white teamsters followed him.

"Terrific," Jessica said softly. "When these men get back to Beaverton they'll spread the word like wildfire. We'll be lucky if we don't have a race war on our hands."

"They were not all Japanese," was all Ki said before he started his horse forward past the wagons and after the vanishing plume of dust. He was right, there, Jessica reflected. She had heard little of the conversation below, but she had heard one man called "Earl," and Earl, whatever he was, had been no oriental—not with that lanky build and the whiskers jutting out from beneath his scarf.

They rode north, veering away from the trail as the outlaws had done, and then followed parallel to the route of the escaping bandits. The wind was cold and gusting out of the north, drifting dust past them, bending the mountain sage that grew profusely among the scattered cedars.

Ahead of them now was a long, low line of hills, slate-gray and jumbled. The dust the outlaws had been stirring up was gone now, dispersed by the wind. Jessie and Ki had no choice but to angle toward the bandits' trail if they weren't going to lose them. And they had no intention of losing them now.

The hills grew larger. Nearly barren, except at the crown where some pines and stunted cedar grew, their flanks were convoluted, flood-scoured, and forbidding.

"Over there," Jessica said, pulling her paint up, pointing eastward toward the hills. At the base of them sat a tumble-down ranch house with three rickety, weather-grayed outbuildings. Two horses, one of them badly swaybacked, were visible in a pole corral. Smoke rose from an iron chimney.

"Let's have a look," Ki said. It was obvious that this wasn't the outlaws' hideout, but maybe whoever lived there knew something of the hills beyond and the riders who emerged from them to execute their raids.

They rode into the weed-filled yard past a broken oak and dry well to the front door of the house. From horseback Ki rapped on one of the porch uprights.

It was a long time before a door opened and a bent little man appeared, half-dressed, a rifle in his hands.

"Get!" he said, gesturing with the rifle.

"We just wanted some help," Jessica said, flashing one of her most brilliant smiles. "We're lost."

"You are, are you?" The old man eyed them suspiciously. He saw some kind of Indian fellow with a blond young lady. They didn't belong out in this country. His brow wrinkled with suspicion. "Who are you, anyway?"

"Just travelers," Ki answered.

"Yeah, sure. Look, traveler. I mind my own business. I know nothin'. I don't take to company. Just ride off and leave me alone."

"Wait," Jessica said as the man turned back toward the door. "We really do need some help." A gold double eagle shimmered in the sunlight as she stretched out a hand toward the hermit rancher. "We'd be willing to pay for directions."

Still the old man was reluctant, but it was obvious from looking around the place that twenty gold dollars would be a small fortune to him. He shrugged, stepped from the porch, and took the gold coin from Jessica's hand, inspecting it before he pocketed it.

"What do you want?" he asked.

"We want to ride through the hills, but we can't find a road."

"You don't want to ride into those hills," the old man said.

"Why not?"

"You don't want to, that's all. If you're looking for a

51

town, Beaverton ain't far off that way." He was still puzzled. These two were traveling light, without even a pair of saddlebags. Something was up, but he couldn't figure what. They sure weren't the law and they didn't seem the type to be on the run.

"We wanted to go through the hills," Ki said. "We're heading east."

"Best thing is to ride around, friend. Fifty miles'll do it."

"I thought there was a town just ahead," Ki tried.

"Nothin' much. Castle Wells ain't hardly a town."

Ki couldn't mask his surprise. Castle Wells. "Walls" was what had been written on the note, but it could very well be the same place—had to be, the name misheard or misspelled by a non-native English speaker.

"That is where we want to go," Ki said evenly. "Castle Wells."

The man shook his head stubbornly. "No, you don't. Believe me."

"What's the matter with Castle Wells? One town's the same as another, isn't it?"

"This one ain't," the man said grimly. He wouldn't say any more about it. He didn't have to. It was obvious that he knew it was an outlaw town. Living on the trail into and out of the hills he would have had to be blind and deaf both not to know what was going on. He survived, it seemed, by keeping his mouth shut.

No matter what Castle Wells turned out to be, Ki was going in there. The outlaws had to be tracked to their lair. And there was Yoshiko.

"Maybe you had better ride back to Beaverton, Jessica," Ki suggested.

"Not on your life. As soon as this fellow earns his twenty dollars by pointing out the trail, we're riding up. Together."

"Bad place for a good woman," the old man said, but that had no effect either. He sighed deeply. "Look, if you got to go, don't take this trail here. Things happen to people along this trail, understand me? A mile or so south

52

you'll see a fan where flash floods've carried rocks and mud off the slopes. Turn up the wash. There's an old Indian trail up that way that takes you in to the back of Castle Wells—in case you want to have a look-see before you ride in."

"Thank you," Ki said.

"You already thanked me." He patted his pocket where the double eagle rested. "If you want to thank me again, do it by staying away from this place. Told you—I don't like company of any kind."

Then he stumped back to the house and entered, slamming the warped door behind him. Jessie and Ki turned their horses' tails to the wind and started riding southward along the foot of the hills.

The alluvial fan was easy to find. Horse-sized boulders had been washed out onto the plains in a sea of mud. Turning up a gully, their horses' hooves crunching the dried mud underfoot, they entered a gradually widening canyon where the wind was cut to a whisper. Sage and manzanita grew in the bottoms, juniper higher up. They found the head of the Indian trail half a mile on, and followed it deeper into the gray hills.

The trail snaked its way up the two-thousand-foot canyon wall toward the windswept crest, where they rested the horses. Jessica removed her hat and wiped back her hair. Ki, holding the reins to his sorrel, squatted, staring back toward the canyon. It was only then that he told Jessica about the note, about Yoshiko.

"It could be a trap," Jessica pointed out.

"Yes, it could be."

And if it was? No matter. They were going in anyway. Why Yoshiko might be at Castle Wells if it was an outlaw town was something beyond Ki just then, but there was certainly something mysterious in the way the people of Beaverton refused even to admit the woman had existed. Maybe it was tied in with the bandits. Maybe.

There was only one way to find out.

They rode on, aiming toward a thin, distant column of smoke, which was no more than a hairline against the pale sky. Jessica had Dancer on her mind still, but beyond that was another, darker thought.

"Back there, Ki," she said, "when they discovered one of the outlaws was Japanese. They were really ugly."

"They are frustrated. They need a target to direct their anger at. Now they think they have found an easily identifiable target."

"You know what could happen after the teamsters get back."

"Racial trouble, you mean? Yes," Ki said with a shake of his head. "But we can do nothing about that but hope that Marshal King handles it properly. We have too much to worry about ourselves just now."

"The outlaw town."

"And," Ki replied, "the men who are following us now."

Chapter 6

They were back there—five of them at Jessica's count. How long they had been there or what their intentions were was anybody's guess.

"Chance?" Jessie said. "There must be others who use this trail from time to time."

"Chance," Ki answered, "or the old man. You buy little loyalty for twenty dollars. Not from a man who depends on the outlaws for his very existence."

"What do we do?"

"Ignore them for now. If they close the distance . . . then we shall have to make another decision."

They dropped down from the hilltop into a shaded glen. More pines surrounded them then and they crossed three or four little brooks. They intersected a second trail which showed signs of travel and turned northward, on a course toward Castle Wells.

It was time for that decision now.

"Ki, they're closing on us," Jessica said, looking behind her to where the five men, their horses lifted to a trot now, had begun serious pursuit. "It looks like they mean business."

Ki had to agree, especially after one of them fired a shot into the air, a puff of smoke rising from his rifle. "What do we do?" Jessica asked.

"Unless you want to surrender"—she shook her head vigorously at Ki's question—"we fight."

Ki yanked his horse's head around and heeled it hard, driving it into the deeper timber, Jessica at his heels. They heard a shout go up from behind them as their followers saw the maneuver and reacted. Ki drew back hard on the reins and leaped from his horse's back almost before it had stopped.

Jessica was off her horse as well, slapping it on the flank to keep it moving for a ways. With her rifle in hand she ran for the shelter of a giant boulder split by the roots of a now-dead oak, and slid up over the sun-warmed rock to sight down the Winchester.

It wasn't long before she had a target. The pursuers had recklessly lifted their horses to a dead run, intent on not losing their quarry. They charged out of the trees dead into Jessica's sights.

Still she held her fire, leaving it up to Ki to make the first move. She could barely see him behind the huge pine where he had hidden himself, but she could see the sunlight through the pines, winking on the bright metal of the throwing stars in his hand.

A moment later someone else spotted Ki. One of the raiders, a red-bearded giant, swung his rifle up and tried a snap shot at Ki. Bark flew from beside the *te* master's head and Ki ducked reflexively. When he came out of his crouch a spinning deadly *shuriken* sang across the space between Ki and the attacker.

The throwing star ripped the throat out of the hired gun and he toppled from his horse, clutching at his throat as he strangled on his own blood.

Angrily the outlaws charged Ki, forgetting that there was another adversary in the forest. Jessie's Winchester spoke twice, the butt bucking against her shoulder, and two outlaws went down.

One of the attackers was suddenly on top of Ki, too close for him to use a *shuriken*. The bay horse he rode seemed ready to trample Ki down. But Ki spun aside, reached up, grabbed the cantle of the outlaw's saddle, and swung aboard behind the outlaw, who tried to turn and thrust his gun into Ki's face.

Ki chopped downward with the side of his hand against the thug's neck and heard a cracking sound. The man fell from the saddle and was dragged along, his boot caught in the stirrup. Behind Ki the last man opened up with a volley of shots.

The samurai felt two bullets thud into the bay's flesh, and the horse went down head over heels as Ki leaped free, came up in a roll, and darted for cover. More bullets pursued him, clipping off low-hanging branches, tearing bark from the trunks of the big trees. Ki saw the fallen log ahead of him and threw himself into a headlong dive as the bullets searched for his flesh.

The outlaw was in hot pursuit—too hot.

His black horse leaped the fallen log as Ki came up, grabbing the horse's foreleg just above the hoof. The horse landed awkwardly and went down hard, rolling over its rider. After a long moment the horse got up, shook its head, and wandered off, dazed.

The rider never got up. His spine had been crushed by the weight of the horse. Ki searched the man's pockets, finding nothing, and then started back toward Jessica. He met her halfway.

Jessica looked him up and down, the concern on her face becoming a smile of relief.

"Come on," she said. Ki swung up behind her and they tracked down Ki's sorrel horse. While Ki adjusted his cinch, Jessie said, "This means they know we're coming, doesn't it?"

"I don't know. If someone sent them, and it wasn't mere coincidence, yes."

"Or if someone heard the shooting, which doesn't seem unlikely. Castle Wells isn't that far off."

"You don't mean you want to go back," Ki said.

"No." She shook her head vigorously. "How can we? But it means I don't like the situation much; do you?"

Ki's answer was a smile. No, he didn't like it at all, but they would go ahead. The outlaw camp was there.

Yoshiko was there.

They returned to the trail long enough to get their bearings, and then veered away from it toward a low rocky knoll with only scattered trees. There they could wait until

57

dark before having a closer look at the town of Castle Wells.

Looking down toward the town Ki could see no one on the trail—maybe a good sign. If the outlaws had heard shooting they likely would have sent more men out to investigate.

"Unless," as Jessica pointed out, "they expected the shots and figured five of their men could handle the two of us."

Ki nodded silently. He had begun measuring the town itself. Twenty buildings, no more, comprised the heart of it. From the west, toward the hills, it was protected by a rough palisade fence. Above and beyond the town was a newer and larger frame building. Long, low, shaped like an L, it followed the contours of the bluff it rested on. The house of the outlaw king? God knew he had stolen enough silver to build himself such a house if he had wanted to.

No one seemed to be on the streets of the town itself, although there were horses tied up in front of a large false-fronted red building, which was presumably a saloon. Ki could hear the sound of a hammer working against metal somewhere.

He glanced at the sky where the sun had begun to sag toward the ragged gray hills and then sat down to wait. After dark they would have their look.

Ki closed his eyes and rested his forehead on his knees and Jessie knew he was asleep. She had wished often enough that she had the ability to do as Ki did and sleep when there was time and need. But she didn't and so she sat awake, watching the valley and the town, thinking about Michael Dancer.

He couldn't be a fake, but he obviously was. That almost surely meant he had to be working for the outlaws. But if he was, why go to all the trouble? Apparently they already had a spy in place. Was Dancer sent just to find out just what Ki and Jessie had in mind? Maybe. She grew tired of thinking about it, but still his half-mocking smile and the touch of his lips against hers returned in memory and she had to force herself to quit thinking about Michael Dancer.

The sun had been down for half an hour before Jessica touched Ki on the shoulder, instantly awaking the *te* master, who stretched his arms and legs in a peculiarly catlike manner before rising.

The night was already cool, the stars bright. The lights had begun to blink on in the town below.

"Which way?" Jessica asked in a whisper.

"There, I think," Ki said, and he nodded toward the white house on the hill. There too lights had begun to twinkle behind curtained windows. "There, if anywhere."

They rode a circuitous route toward the house, their eyes and ears alert to the creatures of the darkness. They saw no one, though—only a startled coyote with a rabbit in its jaws. It loped off into the underbrush at their approach.

The path they followed was little more than a rabbit run, but the stars were bright enough for them to follow it around the shoulder of a rounded hill to a point not a hundred yards above the big house.

From there it looked even larger than it had from across the valley. Ki could see men moving about in the yard—guards, he thought, and it seemed he must have guessed right. The outlaw leader would be the only one who could afford such a place, the only one who would be so well-guarded by armed men.

There were three or four outbuildings behind the house; two of stone, the others of clapboard. There was a light on in one of the wooden buildings—perhaps a bunkhouse of some sort; it was large enough for that. A stand of oaks, perhaps three dozen, massive and dark in the night, stood between the buildings and the main house, where lights blazed in every window.

Once the sound of a human voice drifted to Ki and Jessica, but distance and the wind bent the sound so that they could make nothing out of it.

"What do we do?" Jessica asked.

"What else is there to do?" Ki's voice was grim. "Go on down. *I* will go on down, that is."

"Ki . . ."

"No, this time do not waste objections on me, Jessica Starbuck. This is a job for one person. I am quieter and quicker, and you know it. I only want to see who is here. This is not the time to do battle; nor could we hope to win. You must watch the horses—and if I do not come back, ride to Beaverton and bring Marshal King back here, along with any of Earl Gibbons's men and any of Centennial's people you can bring."

He held her arms as he spoke, looking intently into those sea-green eyes. Jessica's instinct was to argue with the samurai, but this time he was right. Ki was silent as a cat, only a shadow moving across the dark earth when he wanted to be. The job should be his, and she would be only a hindrance to him.

"All right," she sighed. "Damn you, Ki—you'd better watch yourself."

Ki grinned. "I will, I promise you."

With that, he handed Jessica the reins of his horse and was off down the bluff, vanishing into the sage and buckwheat that covered the hillside. Jessica watched for a moment until she could see nothing and then hunkered down to watch the house, shivering a little as the cold wind blew.

For the moment the oaks screened Ki's eyes from the glaring white light from the windows of the big house. He was crouched in the brush, his vision combing the outbuildings and the yard behind the white house. His heart pounded still from the long, snaking run down the hill, and from a healthy warrior's fear. There were, after all, men with guns out there, ready to shoot whatever target presented itself. A man doesn't walk into such situations without feeling a little fear, not even the master warrior, Ki.

He glanced back once toward the bluff, satisfied himself that Jessica was invisible in the darkness, and began working his way forward again.

Ki sprinted silently from the brush to the rear of one of

the dark stone outbuildings, pressing himself against it momentarily as he listened for any approaching sound.

He watched the windows of the big house and once saw someone pass behind a curtain. A woman, he thought, but maybe not. He was thinking first of Yoshiko, and he knew it. He should have been mentally mapping the outlaw town, looking for some evidence as to who was behind all this, perhaps discovering the silver trove if it was stored here—but he was thinking of her . . .

The doe-eyed girl among the jasmine, pretty child, so innocent and yet aware . . .

Ki shook his head. This was getting him nowhere. There was a time to dream, but this wasn't it. He worked his way around the corner of the stone building and drew back sharply. There was an armed guard not ten paces away. If the man had been looking in his direction, it would have been over.

Now Ki heard shuffling bootsteps, and he pressed his back even more firmly against the building, his hands coming up, forming dragon claws. When the guard rounded the corner of the building one of Ki's hands grabbed the barrel of the man's rifle. The other pinched down on nerves and arteries in the outlaw's neck and the man dropped to Ki's feet.

Ki looked around, dragged the man into the brush, and left him there after flinging the rifle away. He started back into the yard, circling this time until he could slip into the trees unseen. Once among the oaks he moved toward the back of the big house. Two guards appeared before him and Ki went softly to the ground.

They were sharing a pint bottle of whisky, shoulders hunched to the wind, muttering the complaints of all soldiers everywhere.

"Damned cold . . . can't even get coffee from the kitchen tonight. Everything's in an uproar after this morning's raid."

"Whoever thought of it was damned smart," the second guard said. "But it won't work again. The boss'll work around it. Give me that damned rye, Jake! Jesus, man, you'll pour it all down!"

They muttered something Ki didn't get, and then something he heard clearly.

"Rather be guarding that Jap bitch. Little thing is something to look at. And it's warm down there."

"I had that duty last night. It wasn't much. Not unless you like getting snake-eyes all night. She just stares. Won't say a word."

"I can't figure what makes her so important anyway," the man called Jake said, taking the whisky bottle again. "Just another Jap bitch."

"I don't know. That's the boss's business," the other guard answered. "I let him do the thinking. He's done all right so far by me."

"Yeah. This is the most money I've had for ten years. Ever, maybe."

The two men moved away in opposite directions after a few more words. Ki rose slowly and followed Jake, who seemed to be heading for the big house—Jake, who knew where Yoshiko was being held. A minute alone with Ki and he would gladly tell all he knew.

Jake was a dozen steps away from a back door. Ki was not far behind when he heard the lever of a Winchester just at his back. Ki halted instantly, even before the man behind him said, "Hold it right there, friend. Jake! You were right. You saw something."

Ki stood, silently cursing himself. Those few muffled words he hadn't quite heard . . . they had seen him and built their little trap. Too anxious to find Yoshiko, he had leaped into it.

The man behind him nudged him once with the muzzle of the rifle he held and Ki put his hands in the air as Jake, reeking of liquor, beaming in triumph, returned to pat Ki's pockets, finding the *shuriken,* which puzzled him, and Ki's knife, which he tucked away behind his belt.

"Let's go, partner," Jake said softly. He was still grinning, and Ki would have liked to kick the grin off his face, but the cocked Winchester was at his back.

"The boss is here?" Ki asked. At least he would have his curiosity satisfied.

"He ain't. That don't matter," Jake snarled.

"The girl? Yoshiko?"

"You may see her sooner than you want," Jake answered. "Come on now, move it. Biff, watch him close. We ain't quite as dumb as you thought, huh, partner?"

"No, not as dumb as I had hoped," Ki admitted quietly. Jake threw back his head and laughed as they walked to the back door, opened it, and entered the big white house.

At least, Ki was thinking as they walked down the narrow paneled corridor, *Jessica knows where I am, and she should be able to make it back to Beaverton to find the marshal.*

"Left, here," Jake said. "Up the stairs."

The stairway was enclosed, the walls painted a dark indefinite color. Far above, a dim light burned. Biff continued to jab Ki in the back with his rifle muzzle. Jake whistled quietly, tunelessly, as they reached the second floor.

Ki noticed that there were no windows along the corridor and only three widely spaced doors. From somewhere the scent of jasmine drifted. Walking across the carpeted floor to the middle door, Jake turned and nodded.

"Stop here. Biff, back off a little. If he spins he'll take that damned Winchester out of your hands before you know what happened."

Jake continued to impress Ki. No, he wasn't half as dumb as Ki would have liked him to be. Jake rapped on the door, and a muffled voice summoned him inside. He ducked his head in, answered, and then nodded to Ki.

"Okay, tall man. Go on in," the outlaw said.

Ki entered the room. It had a low ceiling, deep blue carpeting, and dark furniture. Whoever he expected to see, it wasn't the man behind the desk.

He was short, bald, thick-lipped. He was Japanese, but Ki had never seen the man before.

"This is the one, is it?" the man behind the desk said.

He put a pair of wire-rimmed glasses on, hooking them slowly behind his ears, and rose to come stand before Ki.

He wore a Western business suit in a polished dark blue, a red tie, and a red vest. He came only up to Ki's chest. He circled the *te* master slowly, his pudgy hands clasped behind his back.

"Ki?" he asked.

"Yes. Who are you?"

The response was a sudden and violent kick. The toe of the Japanese's boot slammed into Ki's leg just below the kneecap, and Ki doubled up with pain. The stranger kicked him again, this time in the groin, and Ki folded up, falling to the floor as pain coursed through his body and nausea knotted his stomach.

He lay there peering upward at Jake and Biff, at the bespectacled man, through a haze of pain. "Keep that rifle on him," Ki heard Jake's voice say.

There was further muttered conversation, and then Ki was dragged to his feet. They took him, his legs wobbly, out of the room and back down the stairs. They walked their captive across the large, empty parlor he had seen earlier, and entered a short corridor with a locked oaken iron-strap door at the end of it.

There was a fourth man with them now, though Ki could not remember when he had joined them. His head was clearing and he considered making a move even now, but four was just too many. He could only watch as the iron key was inserted in the lock. The door swung open and then was closed behind him.

It was very damp now, the stone floor irregular. It looked to be the remains of an older building. Older, but even more solid. The walls were of stone, the ceiling heavy beams and oak planking.

"Old French fort was here," Jake said as if reading his thoughts. "They kept renegades and deserters locked up down here. None of them ever got away."

They stopped again, at a door with a small barred window. The keys were produced again. "You're home," Jake said as the door swung open. A solid shove between Ki's shoulderblades sent him staggering into the room.

The woman sat huddled in the corner, the light from a candle lighting her features. The door banged shut behind Ki and he took a step toward her.

"Hello, Yoshiko."

Chapter 7

Her head turned slowly toward Ki and her eyes widened as she came to her feet, stretching out one hand unbelievingly toward the tall man. She wore a torn blue kimono and sandals. Her hair was neatly arranged despite everything. The face glowed with candlelight and sudden joy, but then it faded to distress.

"They have you. It *is* you, but they have you now."

Ki bowed to the young woman. "They have me. Yoshiko—why do they have *you?* I understand so little about this. Sit down." He took her hand and she trembled at his touch. "And tell me about it."

"Yes, yes of course." She looked down at her hand and then up at Ki's face with sheer disbelief in her eyes. "It is really you," she said in a near-whisper.

There were two chairs made from barrels, padded with stuffed sacking, and each of them took one, Ki sitting, hands folded between his knees, to face Yoshiko.

"I dreamed you would come. Come and rescue me, knock them all down, and take me away."

"Yes, like a samurai in a fable," Ki said. "I did not quite accomplish that, did I, Yoshiko?"

"You will . . ." Her hope seemed to fade a little. "Perhaps."

"Perhaps," Ki agreed, forcing a smile. "Start at the beginning, Yoshiko. Why are you here in America?"

"Why!" She seemed almost insulted. "Because"—her eyes dropped—"I wanted to find the man I love. You, Ki."

"You hardly know me, Yoshiko," Ki said gently. "You are only a—"

"Only a child," she snapped. "I know. But I am not, Ki. It was long ago that we walked in the garden. As for my knowing you, I saw your heart that night, and it was a good heart, one to love. I was not with you long, Ki, but it was long enough for me to know you must be my man or I will have none."

Ki started to object, but closed his mouth. Instead he reached out and touched her glossy dark hair. She lifted her eyes hopefully and went on with her story.

"Many of the village people were coming to America. The crops have not been good for several years. First drought, then floods. Most of those who came are here to make money and then go home to begin again on the land."

"The work here is hard."

She smiled. "The work in the rice fields is very hard too, Ki. These people do not mind hard work, so long as they are treated fairly."

"That hasn't exactly been the case, has it?" Ki asked.

"No," Yoshiko said, shaking her head. "But still, things have been bearable for most of us. Yet there were some who used the unfairness in the mine to make trouble."

"The men of the tiger gang," Ki guessed.

Yoshiko was surprised. "Yes. How did you know they were here?"

Ki shrugged. There was no sense in explaining that now.

"It is Takahashi who leads them," Yoshiko said. "Takahashi is a small, round man who shaves his head."

The man upstairs. "I have met him," Ki said drily.

"Have you?" It seemed to Yoshiko that Ki knew everything before she told him. No wonder he was a great warrior. "He is a pig."

"He has hurt you?"

"No; his American boss will not let him touch me."

"His American boss?" Ki's mind shuffled the possibilities. Michael Dancer had risen very high on his list. "What does he look like? What's his name?"

67

"I don't know, Ki. I hear them talk about him, but they will not use his name."

Ki digested the little he knew for a minute. Takahashi had brought over a number of contract thugs to play on the unhappiness of the underpaid and overworked Japanese. An American had either hired Takahashi or agreed to accommodate him. The score was hundreds of thousands in silver.

And the price the innocent paid was going to be paid in blood. The whites in Beaverton were going to be told that the Japanese were behind it and could be expected to strike back in anger over their own lost wages.

"Why are you being held here, Yoshiko? Is it that you know too much about the situation?"

"No, Ki." She looked genuinely astonished. "It is so that Kobi-san will kill you."

It was a long minute before Ki could respond. He sat staring at the young beautiful woman before him, her face fearful and yet flushed with hope in the candlelight.

"He has already tried to kill me," Ki answered. Doubt darkened Yoshiko's features. If her grandfather had tried to kill Ki, he would be dead. The Master did not fail. "It is only chance that kept me alive. Tell me, Yoshiko, why does he want to kill me?"

"Why? They have told him things, Ki. Told him that you have captured me and kept me against my will."

"He believes this of me?" Ki was astonished. Inside he knew that Kobi-san, despite his wisdom, might believe that. His love for his granddaughter could shadow his reason. A threat to her was a threat to Kobi-san's own heart.

"He believes it," Yoshiko said. "Takahashi lied to him. Gave him 'proof.' My necklace. Kobi-san already had a letter from me—the one in which I confessed my love for you." Her voice dropped and again her eyes turned down shyly.

"It is clever, very clever. Why kill me, though? Who could care if I was in Beaverton or not? Who knew about Ki?"

"They knew. About you and . . . a blond woman who owns the mine," Yoshiko responded.

"Jessica, my employer and good friend," Ki said, and Yoshiko brightened at this description of Jessie.

"They did not want her here, or you."

Someone knew they were coming, then, but how? Again, there was no real mystery. In a small town like Beaverton a telegram was a bit of gossip to be shared with everyone.

There was satisfaction in knowing that Jessica would eventually realize that Ki was a prisoner and ride for help. Everything else was decidedly negative at this point. Takahashi had Ki and Yoshiko; what he intended for them was unpredictable. Why wait for Kobi-san to kill Ki when a bullet would do just as well, now that the *te* master was a prisoner? What would happen to Yoshiko then? And to Kobi-san, for that matter? He also was of no further use to this evil consortium of the tiger gang and the Americans.

What American? Gibbons, Strangfeld? Did Dancer enter into it?

"You think deeply, Ki," Yoshiko said, rising.

"Deeply, yes, but not well," he admitted.

"Then do not think; not now," Yoshiko said, and before Ki realized what was happening she was on her knees before him, her hands on his thighs, her cheek resting on his knee.

Ki hesitated and then rested his hand on her head. Yoshiko turned. Her eyes brightened and she suddenly leaped into his arms, clinging to him, kissing him with more exuberance than experience. Ki held her at arm's length, but there was a stirring in his loins nonetheless. He stood and held her, and she wrapped her arms around his waist, hanging on for dear life.

The key in the lock caused Ki to step back and turn.

When the door opened Jessica Starbuck was ushered in and Ki felt his heart drop. Their last hope was gone. It was over. Takahashi and his American master had won.

69

Jessica's face was smudged, her hat missing, her blouse split at the shoulder seam. She just shook her head at first, looking at Yoshiko without apparent surprise.

"Sorry, Ki," she said finally. "I got careless."

"Apparently," Ki replied quietly. "I also was careless. Nothing can be done about it now. Are you all right?"

"All right." Jessica sighed, looked at the bunk bed, and sagged onto it.

Yoshiko was staring at Jessica. Apparently this wasn't what she had expected to see if and when she saw the female American mine owner.

"What do you think, Ki?" Jessie asked. "What've we walked into and what are they going to do with us?"

Briefly Ki explained what Yoshiko had told him and what he had deduced. "The idea was to steal silver, of course, but also to cause trouble between the Japanese and native Americans."

"For what reason?"

"I would guess that it was with an eye toward taking over the mine. What use is a mine that can't show a profit?"

"I see. And since we wanted to find solutions, they wanted us out of the way."

"Of course. They went so far as to bring Kobi-san here to kill me. Now, that is unnecessary."

Yoshiko said, "They will kill us!"

"No," Ki said with a smile, but his glance at Jessica admitted that he had no hope things would be different.

"Michael Dancer?" Jessica asked almost hopefully.

"I don't know. He doesn't fit. He's obviously not the man Pearson sent, but still . . ."

"You don't believe he's the gang leader."

Ki grew cautious. "I haven't enough information to make a judgment, Jessica."

Yoshiko didn't know who Dancer was. She had her own more immediate concerns. "What can we do now? We can't let them kill us."

"No. We must try to escape," Ki said. He looked at the

70

barred door, knowing just how difficult a task that would be.

"You have an idea?" Yoshiko was beaming again, having a lot of faith in the abilities of her dream warrior.

"None good enough," Ki answered honestly.

"It'll have to be soon, Ki, if we try it," Jessie pointed out. "They haven't got a reason in the world to keep us hanging around."

"Perhaps they need permission from the American boss," Ki said thoughtfully. "I don't know. But you're right, they can't let us stay alive for long."

They fell into silence then as the candle burned down in the gloomy room. An hour later food was brought to the cell. Ki watched the men closely, his eyes intent, his body coiled, but they gave him no opportunity at all to strike. One man, unarmed, entered the room while another with a shotgun waited in the hall, covering them. Any move would have meant risking the lives of Jessie and Yoshiko, with buckshot spraying the room.

They ate silently. Ki couldn't even tell what it was they had been given. Some sort of corncakes fried in pork grease. He ate only to keep his strength up. If he was to have a chance at escape, he would need that.

"Eat up," was the last thing the guard said. "Never can tell when a meal's your last."

He found that very amusing and laughed all the way out the door and down the hall. Ki stared at the closed door, vowing to find some way out of there.

Even if that were possible, however, he was skeptical; they would be afoot in outlaw territory, miles from help, unarmed. Was it even *possible* to escape from these people? Even if they left the cell door open?

Silently he ate, glancing from time to time at the women: Jessica had been in tighter places, but she still looked worried. Yoshiko resigned to it all, still hopeful that her samurai would break them out of here.

"Any ideas yet, Ki?" Jessica asked after they were through with the revolting meal.

"None without risk involved."

"Then," she said simply, "we'll have to take a risk." She too glanced at Yoshiko. "We sure as hell can't stay here and wait for them to do what they want to do."

"No." Ki shook his head. "We can't wait."

"Tear the door from its hinges!" Yoshiko burst out. Ki didn't know whether to smile or groan. Was *that* the image the woman had of him? A man with superhuman powers, invincible?

"There is another way," he said soothingly. That seemed to satisfy her for the moment. Just what other way was still a mystery to Ki himself. He looked again at Jessica and shrugged.

"You don't want to tear the door off?" Jessica asked, a smile playing around her lips.

Ki wasn't amused. He smiled anyway. Jessica was only trying to lighten up a situation that was nearly desperate.

"When?" she asked more quietly.

"At the next meal."

"How? You saw how they handled it."

"I saw," Ki replied. There wasn't confidence in his voice so much as determination. They might live until the next meal, and then again they might not. It was a certainty that they wouldn't last much longer than that, not after the American boss was contacted and gave the word to go ahead with the executions. And what other decision could the man reach? Jessica Starbuck and Ki had to die. Yoshiko was no longer of any use. They had to take a long chance. Or die where they sat.

Ki gave Jessie some idea of what he had in mind. Yoshiko was deliberately left out of it, although she sat staring at Ki with eyes filled with admiration. She simply didn't have the skills to help out.

Guessing when the next meal might come was impossible. They could only sit there in their small dark prison and wait, lifting their heads at every sound.

When they finally did hear bootheels ringing on the stone flooring beyond their cell's walls, there wasn't even a way of knowing if they were going to be fed again or taken to the executioner.

72

No matter—they had to try something, and now.

Ki put his finger to his lips and rolled under the cot next to the wall. The key was in the lock and turning. Jessica sat on one of the barrel chairs, her head hanging. Yoshiko looked apprehensive, but she didn't look Ki's way. That much had been impressed upon her.

Again the unarmed guard entered the room while the man with the double-ten shotgun stood in the doorway, eyes narrowed and watching.

The man with the tray started to put it down, and then paused, his mouth tightening. He looked around the room and glanced back at his partner.

"The big Jap—where is he?"

His answer wasn't long in coming. Ki's hands shot out from under the bunk and grabbed his ankles, yanking hard. The man went down with the tray, spattering food everywhere. His head hit the solid stone floor with a solid *thunk*, and he was out.

The guard with the shotgun charged into the room, cocking the weapon. Ki rolled away again, but the guard smiled. That would do the son of a bitch no good. Not when that load of buckshot ripped the bed apart.

He was so busy gloating over Ki's anticipated murder that he never saw the young blonde rise from her barrel chair, whirl, and deliver a sidekick to his shotgun. The weapon went flying and, as the guard spat out a muffled curse, Jessica kicked him again, in the groin, and he folded up.

Still, he was a tough one. He reached out for her, taking her by the hair, yanking her to him. By that time Ki had rolled out from under the bed again, and a downward chop of the *te* master's hand knocked the thug unconscious. He toppled forward with an audible sigh and lay still on top of his partner.

"Now, let's go!" Ki said, yanking Yoshiko to her feet.

Jessica had already recovered the shotgun, and now she peered out into the hallway, which was dark and empty for the moment.

"It's all right," she whispered over her shoulder to Ki.

Ki had Yoshiko by the arm. He half pulled, half led her to the door. Ki glanced at Jessica meaningfully and then at her shotgun. It was going to be hell fighting their way through the house and back up the bluff, and they both knew it.

"Wait!" Yoshiko was breathless as Ki tugged her down the hallway. "There is another door at the far end. Would it be safer?"

It couldn't be any worse. Ki looked down the corridor, unable to see its end in the poor light. "You are sure?"

"They've taken me out that way—to let me walk and get fresh air."

"All right. We'd better try it."

Ki went first, gliding across the stone floor, Jessica and Yoshiko moving at a trot behind him. Opening the door was no problem. A heavy bolt on the inside slid back easily, and Ki, holding his breath, opened the door a crack, peering out into the dark exterior.

Jessica touched his shoulder and he glanced at her. "I don't see anyone," he said.

Which, as they both knew, meant nothing. There could have been a hundred men hidden out there in the oak grove. Still there was nothing to do but chance it. Ki slipped out, went to one knee, and let his eyes scan the darkness more carefully. Jessie was suddenly behind him and Yoshiko, her breathing audible and rapid in the night.

Ki pointed a finger toward the low stone wall to their left and started that way, half expecting gunshots in the night. He achieved the wall without trouble, leaped it, and helped to lift Yoshiko over as Jessica rushed to join them. For a minute they waited, catching their breath. Then, at a nod from Ki, they circled toward the oaks, moving cautiously toward the stone bunkhouse. Once behind it they meant to make their way upslope again toward the back trail out of Castle Wells.

It didn't work that way.

★

Chapter 8

A guard appeared from behind the stone building and ran into Ki's foot. Ki's high kick struck the outlaw on the chin, snapping his head back sharply. The rifle in his hand discharged as an involuntary twitch of his finger squeezed off the round in the Winchester's chamber. The stab of flame seared Ki's face as the bullet whined off into the distance, drawing men from the night like homing bees.

The second man was no more fortunate. He burst from the oaks, his rifle raised overhead like a club. Ki blocked the downward blow intended for his skull and struck back with a *nakadate* blow, a middle-knuckle punch to the outlaw's diaphragm. The bandit dropped to the ground writhing in pain.

Jessica had yanked Yoshiko back behind the big oak to her left as the outlaws rushed toward them. A big man in a duster ran right past them and Jessie stuck out her foot, sending the outlaw sprawling. Before he could get up Jessica kicked him in the back of the head and he went down to stay.

By then Ki had caught up with the two women and he led them off through the trees. They ran upslope through the brush, hearing shouts behind them, and one shot— aimed at ghosts it seemed, since it came nowhere near them.

They reached the trail above the house and Yoshiko sagged to her knees, gasping for breath. Jessica, holding her own chest, asked breathlessly, "Which way now, Ki?"

His idea had been to follow the trail back through the hills, but now, glancing that way, he could see torchlight.

They were already searching for them in that direction. That left one way out of the hidden valley.

"Through town."

"Ki!"

"I know it sounds crazy, but there is no other way." Takahashi's people wouldn't expect them to go through the outlaw town; and there was a chance they could find some horses there—horses they desperately needed if they were going to make their run a successful one.

When Yoshiko was able they started down again, circling wide of the searchers below. Now and then they could hear voices raised—shouting in two languages. But none of them were near enough to pose a threat.

The real threat lay ahead in the form of a town built for and inhabited by outlaws. Ki considered changing his plan as they neared Castle Wells, but there wasn't any other real choice. On foot they would have no chance at all of escaping from the valley and making it across the plains to Beaverton.

Maybe Takahashi had no further use for Yoshiko, but he couldn't allow the Centennial mine owner and her bodyguard to continue snooping, to continue fighting back against the silver thieves.

Nor could the American boss. That still bothered Ki. Just who was he?

They slipped into the little town from the north end, making their way down rubbish-strewn alleys. Every other building seemed to house a saloon or a whorehouse. More than once they passed drunks, passed out in the alleys.

"There must be a stable somewhere," an exasperated Jessica said.

"There must be," Ki agreed, but they hadn't spotted one yet. That left the alternative—taking some mounts from one of the hitchrails in front of a saloon. It wasn't a hell of an appealing idea, but Ki had none better just then.

Yoshiko gasped and gripped his arm when he told the women what he had in mind. "You will be killed."

"We will all be killed if we don't find some horses," Ki answered. He noticed the soft glow in Yoshiko's eyes even as she pretended to fear for his life. She was thrilled by the night's activity, by the prospect of more danger. Yoshiko was a child in the world, dwelling in her own make-believe world of maidens and ever-victorious samurais.

"Do you want a diversion, Ki?" Jessica asked.

That wasn't a bad idea, but as long as they were at it, why not make it more than a diversion? Ki told Jessie what he had in mind and she agreed, a smile slowly forming on her lips.

Ki let Jessie and Yoshiko start off toward the south end of town while he waited, crouched in the darkness, listening to the street noises. He already had his eye on the hitchrail across the street. Two men stood on the porch of the saloon, drinking whisky, playing some sort of game with their knives. He could only hope that Jessie's diversion drew them off.

Of one thing there was no longer any doubt: A good portion of the gang Takahashi was running were Japanese. Now and then Japanese, dressed for the most part in Western clothing, passed the head of the alley, their language laced freely with American cusswords.

There were a hundred men in town at least—a huge gang, but then, there was enough silver to meet any payroll. How Marshal King, or anyone short of the army, was going to attack this nest of thieves, was a large problem.

Ki heard the flames before he saw them. He looked to the south, watching the first bright tongue of flame leap into the sky. He smiled to himself.

Jessica never saw the first fire start. She was already to a second building—some sort of warehouse of gray, weathered wood—splashing it with what was left of the can of kerosene she had found behind the first building.

The match was a small, winking flame which leaped to life as it touched kerosene. Smoky flame rose into the night sky above the outlaw town. Yoshiko, her face glowing in the firelight, stepped back from the heat and clapped her hands.

"Come on," Jessica said, taking her hand. "It won't take them long to come running."

Less than a minute was what Ki figured—from the time he first saw the flames until men burst from the saloons and started charging down the street, some with firebuckets in hand.

Ki let the first wave of outlaws run past him and then joined the milling mob on the street. He was within three steps of the horses when someone recognized him for a stranger.

A black-bearded, broken-nosed man leaped toward him and Ki spun and crouched, coming up with a *yonhonnukite* blow followed by a sharp chop to the outlaw's neck.

The man caved in, but there was a roar from the outlaws in the street. Ki, slipping the reins of the three horses, heeled the pony he had mounted away from the rail, going to its side as the blast of a .44 sent lead whipping past his head.

The horses pounded up the street, bullets pursuing them. Ki was nearly past the alley where Yoshiko and Jessicas had taken shelter before Jessie leaped out, waving her hands.

Ki brought the horses up sharply as Jessie half threw Yoshiko onto the back of a black gelding and herself mounted the long-legged roan. Bullets still whined past them, although the outlaws, at a distance now, didn't have much chance of hitting anything.

But there was always the chance.

Ki heeled his stolen horse again sharply and led the dash up the street. From the fire-swamped buildings more gunmen emerged to level Colt revolvers at the hard-riding invaders. In a moment, however, Ki and the women were past the bandits and into the darkness of the surrounding hills.

Ki slowed his horse just a little. "They'll be waiting in the pass, Jessica!" he shouted.

The fire and the following shots would have alerted the outlaws in the pass beyond that something was wrong. Probably the word had already reached them that some outsiders had entered the valley. Now the pass would be closed down tight. The road to the south, they already knew, was blocked by searchers.

"Which way?" Jessie called back.

"North?" It was just that—a question. Which way was there to go? They knew nothing of the country to the north —whether there was another pass out of the valley, whether it too was guarded. The only certain thing was that they couldn't remain where they were. The distant, pursuing thudding of hoofbeats left no doubt about that in their minds.

"North."

It was an hour before they could no longer see the bright glow of fire against the leaden skies, an hour of winding through the rock-strewn brushy country before Ki finally decided they had lost their pursuers.

Not that any of them felt secure. They were in unfamiliar country at night, surrounded by men who wanted their hides. The scattered clouds had begun to merge into a thick cloud cover, obscuring the stars. The moon was late rising these nights, and had been nothing more than a narrow, dim crescent anyway.

We'll have to find a place to hole up, Ki thought. Yoshiko looked dismayed when he said it.

"Where?" She looked around at the dark and alien land, and to the cold skies.

"We'll have to do the best we can. It won't do to break a horse's leg or ride into an outlaw patrol. High ground," he answered, looking up. "Outside of that we'll have to take our chances."

They climbed higher then, riding a game trail by the feeble starlight. When Ki finally halted them, it was on a windswept ridge high above the valley. From there they could look back and see Castle Wells and, across the foothills, the far distant glow of Beaverton, a seemingly impossible distance away.

It was cold and the wind gusting over their bodies made it still colder, yet on the sheltered side of the ridge, where a great fan-shaped rock curled up over them, it was possible to stay out of the cutting wind. The horses, hobbled and

79

put out to graze in the scant buffalo grass, seemed satisfied. Ki, Yoshiko, and Jessica, huddled together behind the rock, were warmer, and safer than they had been for hours —for Yoshiko it had been much longer.

Held prisoner by Takahashi, she had been in fear for her life, alone and cold for weeks. Now, slowly, the tension drained out of her. She had her freedom and her samurai. Her hand rested on Ki's leg as her head rolled to his shoulder.

"I'm not afraid," she said, lifting her eyes, "so long as you are here."

"I am here," Ki answered, "for now. But you must understand me, Yoshiko. When we return to Beaverton you must find Kobi-san and go home."

"I wish to stay with you."

"No." Ki shook his head and said in Japanese, "It cannot be."

"I will be loyal, faithful, loving . . ." Yoshiko began, using the same language. Ki cut her off.

"It cannot be." Then in English, "Jessie, I'll stand watch while you two sleep."

"Think someone's back there still?"

"I don't think we want to risk it," Ki answered. He rose and picked up the shotgun Jessie had been carrying. Ki didn't like firearms much, but he knew how to use them as well as any man, and this might be the place for one.

Yoshiko's hand touched his leg as he walked away into the darkness, searching for a vantage point. Alone in the night, Ki breathed in deeply and stood watching the back trail, the dark silhouettes of their horses against the sky. He saw nothing, heard no sound; but he wasn't automatically discounting the possibility of there being eyes, ears, and deadly weapons in the hills. Ki had seen too much danger, fought too long, to make such assumptions.

He found a stone outcropping which still held the warmth of the day and eased out onto it. Eight feet by twenty, it overhung the trail they had used to reach the summit. It gave Ki a good view of almost the entire valley, and he stood there for long minutes searching it with his eyes before he settled cross-legged to the rock to begin his long watch.

When she came her hair was down, her kimono open. As Ki rose she stepped into his arms, wrapping her slender arms around his waist.

"Yoshiko . . ." Ki objected.

"I am no longer a child, Ki. I know the secret ways. Let me show you."

The kimono dropped to the rock to lie in a soft silken wreath at her feet, and Yoshiko stepped back briefly to allow Ki to admire her beauty. Firm, uptilted breasts, narrow waist, flaring hips, slender legs.

"You are right," Ki admitted. "You are no longer a girl."

Yoshiko laughed softly and stepped to Ki, her fingers going to his belt buckle, her lips touching his throat. The wind was still cool, but the rock was warm. As they lay against it on a bed made of their clothing, Yoshiko climbed on top of Ki, who rested on his back against the stone.

She bent low to kiss him and her long, soft hair fell across his shoulders and throat. Ki's arm looped around her neck and tugged her down to meet his kiss.

Yoshiko might have believed she knew the secret ways of love, but nothing she had learned had prepared her for the trembling Ki's kiss sent through her body. She sighed and sagged against him, holding herself still for a moment before her fingers began tracing patterns across Ki's shoulders, sliding down his side to his thighs and then between his legs.

She gasped audibly. Her training had not prepared her for this either, not for solid man-flesh encountered outside of her lessons. It sent a thrill through her as she wrapped her fingers tentatively around Ki's shaft.

"So," she said, and she gave a little nod.

Ki smiled up at her, kissed her once more, and let his own hands run down the sleek flanks of the young woman, his fingers tracing the lines of her ass as her legs slowly parted.

Yoshiko sat up and Ki let his eyes feast on her slender

shape. He reached for her breasts and toyed with the taut, dark nipples. Yoshiko let her head loll back on her neck. She gazed at the sky, eyes closed, and let sensation become her entire world as Ki's hands searched her body and his swollen man-flesh throbbed between her legs.

Without warning she lifted herself and inserted Ki into the warm depth of her body, taking him in with some effort. With a deal of eagerness, she settled to the root of his shaft with a little wriggle and a satisfied whispery sound. After a moment of sitting perfectly still again, letting her body adjust to him, she began to sway against Ki, her hips moving in a circular motion.

"Do I do right? " she asked as she reached between her own thighs to touch Ki where he entered her.

"Very right," Ki answered honestly. His hands ran up her arms and gripped her shoulders as she continued to work against him, all of the tentativeness gone now as her body found the ancient primal rhythm of sex.

Ki arched his back and Yoshiko gasped as he penetrated even farther. With a sudden soft cry Yoshiko bent forward, bracing herself with unsteady arms. She lifted her body and looked back between her legs, fascinated by the act, by the slow entrance and withdrawal of Ki's solid rod.

Ki could feel her begin to tremble. He gripped her ass tightly for a moment, holding her perfectly still as the trembling increased. Her breath was coming in rapid puffs now as she looked into his eyes and fell against him, her body taking on urgent motion as she drove her pelvis against him frantically.

Ki could feel the need for release building in his loins. The girl was lovely, her body lithe and beautiful. Her hips worked their magic.

Yoshiko came with a muffled shout. Her eyes, starry before, grew astonished—astonished at her own womanhood, which she had finally met. Ki held her very still. When he thrust against her again it was a small movement, but the one that triggered his body to a sudden rush of sensation. He climaxed as Yoshiko, shuddering, clung to him, her fingers kneading his shoulders and neck, touching his thighs and hard-muscled chest with amazement.

"And so," she asked later as Ki held her, stroking her back, "I did it not so bad."

"Not so bad." Ki kissed her ear and tugged her kimono over her. The night was still chilly, and as thier bodies cooled they could feel it again. Ki was totally relaxed, fulfilled. He wanted nothing more than to sleep in Yoshiko's arms that night, but there was nothing more dangerous than that; the outlaws were still out there somewhere. They couldn't afford to assume that they had lost their trail.

"Now," Ki said, touching her ear with the tip of his finger, "you must go back and sleep by Jessica."

"I don't want to, Ki."

"No, but you must. This is not safe. It was foolish in many ways."

"You regret it?" she asked, half sitting up.

"No," he answered after a moment. "I regret it not at all." He kissed her again and then patted her rump. "Now, do as I tell you and dress."

"Yes, Ki," she answered submissively.

Ki was silent then, pulling on his own clothing as he looked down at the dark valley. Yoshiko touched his arm.

"What is it, my warrior?" she asked him. "What is troubling you now? Is it something I did?"

"No, nothing. I was thinking only of Kobi-san. What would your grandfather say about this?"

"He would say nothing, Ki," Yoshiko answered brightly. "He would only kill you."

"Yes," Ki replied grimly. "Only kill me."

But then the Master already had that in mind, believing that Ki had stolen Yoshiko. At least, Ki thought, they would not encounter Kobi-san out here in the hills. He was an old man, too old to be roving the countryside pursuing an adversary. Kobi-san would be waiting in Beaverton, waiting and watching for Ki and his next opportunity to kill his former student.

With a brief kiss Yoshiko left him, her hand falling

away from his arm. Ki watched her fade into the darkness, finished dressing, and turned to take up his post again.

"Sorry," Michael Dancer said. "Didn't mean to break in."

Ki tensed, automatically crouched to assume a stance. Dancer laughed softly.

"Ki, there's no need for that."

"Where have you come from? Where have you been?" Ki asked, his eyes staying on the right hand of Dancer, which hung near his holstered Colt revolver. The wind lifted Dancer's fine hair, and that grin was in place, but Ki knew, if he hadn't known before, that Dancer was a dangerous man. No matter the distraction, Ki should have heard someone approaching his position. He hadn't heard Dancer.

Behind Ki, footsteps sounded and he turned his head that way. Jessica Starbuck appeared from out of the night, long hair drifting. "Ki—" she began, but her words broke off suddenly. "Dancer!"

"That's right, Jessie," the tall man said. "I've come back to straighten things out."

Then Dancer drew his pistol.

Chapter 9

Jessica's eyes were fixed on the big blued single-action Colt Michael Dancer had drawn, and on the crouching, tensed Ki. Dancer, amazingly, was still grinning. He reversed the pistol suddenly and tossed it to Jessica, who caught it awkwardly.

"You've got the firepower now," Dancer said. "How about talking things over?"

Jessie didn't bother to cock or aim the weapon. A man who means to kill you doesn't hand his gun over. The grin was genuine, if impenetrable.

"We'd better talk, yes," Ki answered. "Who are you, Dancer? What in hell are you up to?"

"I'm just an employee of Starbuck Enterprises, " Dancer said, crouching down, his elbows resting on his knees. "A man trying to do a job for the boss here."

"Is that right?" Jessica said with some irony. "Working for Pearson, right?"

"That's right," Dancer said amiably. He had picked up a small twig and was scratching in the dust with it.

"We wired Pearson. The investigator he sent is a man named Jack Troupe, a former federal marshal," Jessica said.

"I know it. I know all about Troupe, and all about Strangfeld and his operation, Miss Starbuck."

Jessica glanced at Ki. It made no sense to either of them. "Put it on the line, Michael," she said.

"Sure. Pearson was asked to send an investigator down here. Jack Troupe's the usual man for that job. He's been around and knows his business."

"Then . . ."

"The trouble is, no one told the boss that Troupe and Strangfeld were old friends. They did time in the Texas Rangers together. Not that that means anything, but you know how it goes—friends looking into the affairs of other friends. Pearson decided to send me tagging along just to be sure."

"When we wired him—"

"When you wired him, he had enough sense not to answer fully. Jessica, you know how word leaks out of that telegraph office. You know how effective I would be if my name popped up again. There's that, and the more obvious fact that anyone in the world could send a telegram to Pearson and sign it 'Jessica Starbuck.' With the problems we've had down here, Pearson wasn't taking any chances. He told you the truth, but not quite all of it."

Ki asked, "Where is Jack Troupe?"

Dancer shook his head. "Wish I knew. He could be anywhere, undercover, beside the trail somewhere, or down a mineshaft. I haven't been able to turn him up. It looks to me like he's been eliminated."

Ki looked at Jessie as if to ask, "Do you believe all of this?" But it was obvious from the relief in her eyes that she did. Dancer hadn't proved a thing to Ki, but Jessica's instincts said the man was telling the truth, and she was seldom wrong.

She tossed the Colt back to him and Dancer holstered it. "All right—where'd you disappear to, Michael?"

"Don't know for sure," Dancer said. "I was up at the mine poking around and someone decided to use my head for an anvil." He fingered his scalp gingerly. "I vaguely remember fighting someone off and crawling away into some trees. Next thing I knew it was daylight and you were gone, the silver shipped out, my head ringing away like brass bells."

"You tracked us here," Ki said. "How?"

"I wanted to see Castle Wells for myself. Someone told me there was a lot of unusual activity up here. Found a little crest trail and came into the valley. Heard some shooting and sat and watched." he shrugged. "Nothing much to it."

There was a lot to it, Ki thought. In the darkness it took a hell of a tracker to figure out what was going on, and then follow a difficult trail over broken country. Ki had been right about one thing—Dancer was a dangerous man.

They could only hope that he was telling the truth, that he was on their side.

"Jessie?" Ki asked.

After a pause she said, "I believe him." She proved it by handing Dancer the bullets she had taken from the cylinder of his .44.

"This trail you entered the valley on," Ki asked, "can you find it again?"

"Sure."

"Is it safe to ride out on, do you think?"

Dancer could only shrug. "That's anyone's guess now. Maybe the outlaws have closed it off, I don't know. When I rode in, it was unguarded. That doesn't mean it is now. Want to try it?"

"Have we a choice?" Ki asked.

"No. Not much of one."

"Can we find it again now?"

"I think so," Dancer said. "We'd better try, don't you think? Daylight will find the outlaws fanned out everywhere."

"We'd better try. I'll get the horses," Ki said.

Jessica picked up the ten-gauge, which rested where Ki had left it, and stood facing Dancer for a while. "Buster," she said, "you'd better be playing straight with us this time."

Dancer's answer was brief. He looped one arm around Jessica's waist and drew her to him, kissing her parted lips hard before releasing her. When he stepped back he was grinning.

"Hell, Jessie—how could you not trust a man like me?"

They caught up with Ki and helped him saddle up. Dancer's own horse, he said, was not far up the trail. While he went to get it, Ki went to wake Yoshiko from her brief but very deep sleep. When she sat up she threw her arms around Ki and murmured to him dazedly.

"Again, my samurai?"

"No. We have to move on now, Yoshiko. A friend's come. He knows a way out of the valley."

"A friend?"

"You'll meet him later. Get on your feet now, pin up your hair. We have to be riding."

Back at the horses, Ki was handed a rifle by Dancer. "Thought maybe you'd feel better with one of these in your hands."

Ki took it. The *shuriken* he had been carrying had been confiscated by Takahashi's men, and his others were back in the Beaverton hotel room. Yoshiko, still somewhat dazed by the lovemaking and lack of sleep, clung to her horse. She was obviously no rider.

"Ready?" Dancer asked.

"Ready," Jessica answered. Hell, yes, she was ready—to get out of this valley and raise an army to ride back and destroy Castle Wells. Takahashi, she thought, would talk quick enough once he was arrested, and that would finish the gang for good.

Dancer immediately got them lost, leading them up a blind canyon. He cursed and apologized and led them out again. "Maybe I'm not going to have any luck at this in the dark. From the other side everything looks different."

They started around the shoulder of a low split mountain and nearly rode into a roving outlaw patrol.

Ki saw the horses, only dark smudges against the dark background, and he touched Jessie's shoulder, whistling softly to Dancer, who reined up and looked around, puzzled. Ki jabbed a finger ahead of them.

The outlaws were three hundred feet or so below them, climbing toward them, perhaps seeking the hidden pass themselves. Ki swung down and walked his horse into the brush, clamping his hand over the animal's muzzle to keep it from blowing as it scented the other horses.

Dancer was crouched beside his horse, pistol in hand. Jessie was ready with the shotgun. If it turned into a firefight it would be nasty. Behind Ki and Jessie a stone bluff rose sharply. They were virtually trapped in there. They could hear voices now, muffled and bent by the wind.

". . . find nobody in the damn dark . . ."

"Shut up. That's what we're paid for."

Another, higher-pitched voice complained, "I'm not shootin' a woman anyway. It ain't done."

"It's done—when the pay is right."

The first of the horses appeared in front of them. Ki crouched lower, peering up through the screen of greasewood and sage, his rifle dangling loosely but already cocked in his hand as he steadied his horse.

"Don't see what the difference is," one of the outlaws said. "Say they get back to Beaverton. So what? We can take 'em there just as easy."

"They got a telegraph is the difference, you dumb shit," a second man growled.

There was some more grumbling and cursing and then the outlaws were gone, swallowed up by the night. Ki whispered to Dancer.

"The pass? Think they're heading for it?"

Dancer was uncertain. "I don't think so," he said finally. "It seems to me it's farther south still."

"Then where?" Jessica asked.

"I don't know," Ki interrupted. "But let's start riding before one of them opens his eyes enough to see our tracks on the trail."

There was a chance of that now. The sliver of a moon had broken through the broken, drifting clouds, and although it was far from bright still, visibility was better than it had been by far. It might be of a help in finding the pass, but then again, it might keep them from ever reaching it at all.

The trail dipped down after that, for which Ki was grateful. It kept them off the skyline at least, making it harder for any watchers to spot the four horses and their riders.

There were three more false trails before Dancer found the one leading to the high pass. They halted at the foot of the pass, looking upward. Three or four hundred feet higher they could see the notch in the hills through which the trail passed before dropping down again to the plains beyond.

"They could be there," Jessica said. "It's a natural if they know about it."

"They'll know," Ki said grimly.

"What do you want to do, Ki?" Dancer asked finally.

"I want to go ahead and take a look around."

"Alone?"

"It is the only way."

"Better let me . . ."

Ki's answer came in the form of a rifle, which he tossed to Dancer before slipping from his horse, handing the reins to Jessie. "This will be better," he said from the ground. "Believe me."

"Ki, there could be three or four gunmen up there," Dancer objected, starting to swing down himself.

"Yes, there could be," Ki answered mildly. "Still, I will go alone, Dancer."

"Crazy." Dancer looked to Jessica. "He's crazy. Tell him to let me go along. He'll get himself killed."

"No," Yoshiko said tranquilly. "He will not be killed. He is the great samurai, the invincible warrior."

Dancer looked at all of them as if they'd gone mad. Finally, shaking his head, he settled back into the saddle to wait and watch as Ki sifted off through the shadows toward the stony notch above them.

The trail was steep but Ki jogged on easily, following the dusty trail upward. He kept his eyes on the crest, and when he judged it was time for more caution, he veered from the trail and scrambled up a rocky bank. The watchers—if there were any—would be expecting them to arrive on horseback, and that meant guarding the trail below. There wasn't much to watching, just listening for horses in the night in this deserted area. It required little attention to hear four horses laboring up the road, even at night. The watchers would be careless, lazy, cold.

Or so Ki hoped.

Up over a fallen cedar and through a patch of nopal cactus, where he picked up a scratch or two, Ki jogged. He was actually above the notch in the hills now. The moon showed his way clearly and illuminated the land below with feeble but adequate light.

He slowed his pace now that he was nearer. His heart thumped heavily in his chest and his breathing was a little ragged. At the crest of a crumbling ridge he paused, crouched, and watched. He could see nothing, hear nothing.

And then he did.

A horse whickered from out of the darkness, and a low curse followed. Ki's eyes shifted, seeking the source of the sounds. At last he saw what he had been looking for and he smiled to himself.

The bandits had chosen their spot well. Above the trail itself was a narrow, two-sided alcove where their tiny fire could remain hidden. Ki himself hadn't seen it at first, even from above, but now he saw the pale, reflected light of the fire on the stone walls. A man, like a stick figure at that distance, was walking across the alcove toward the larger figure of a horse.

One man? No—two, Ki saw now. Another stood and stretched, holding the small of his back as he did so. A word or two passed between the men. Ki began to work his way behind them.

The outlaws spoke in low voices, but Ki paid no attention to what they were saying. All of his concentration was focused on the physical—the posture of his own body, the positions of the two men, the distance between himself and them, the height of the drop.

Perched ten feet above them on a foot-wide ledge, Ki waited until the man to his left had poured himself a cup of coffee and turned his back. Then he pounced like a big cat, dropping through the space between himself and the outlaws, landing just beside the low burning fire.

"Hey!" The man with the coffee cup yelled out, dropping his cup as he tried to grab for his holstered pistol. Ki's leaping *tobi-geri* kick sent the man flying into the fire, spraying sparks and ash everywhere.

The second outlaw had come up with his rifle. Ki, spinning, kicked the rifle from the man's hands and thrust toward his heart with a *choku-zuki* blow—short, deadly, pulled just enough to stun the outlaw without stopping his heart.

Ki wiped back his hair and dragged the first man from the fire, patting out his smoldering clothes. Then he bound both of them with their own belts and scarves and started back down the trail toward Jessie and the others.

He whistled once softly before emerging from the shadows. There was always the possibility of being taken out by an over-anxious shot.

When he went forward again he found the three of them in a half-circle, waiting. Dancer slowly lowered his weapon and grinned. Yoshiko rushed into his arms and said triumphantly over her shoulder, "You see, I told you no one could harm the great warrior, Ki."

"We'd better keep moving," Jessie said more practically. "No telling who's behind us."

"You are right," Ki answered, prying Yoshiko from him. "Get your horse, woman."

Jessica's head came around sharply. Ki didn't talk to women, *any* women, in quite that tone. He was above all a gentleman. Perhaps, she decided, he cared too much for Yoshiko, and was trying to hide it.

She had little time to think about it. They rode in single file up the mountain trail, the moon seeming to follow them from behind the sheer silver clouds. All of Jessica's attention was on the shadows, the brush beside the road, and the highlands, where more outlaws might be concealed.

They rode through the notch and Dancer took the lead, guiding them confidently now down a winding trail among huge, stacked boulders, which cast mysterious shadows.

In another hour they were onto the plains and riding steadily toward Beaverton. Jessie thought the game was nearly won. They would report the gang's location and ride back with whatever posse Marshal King could raise. The miners, she thought, would be happy to help out in eliminating the bandits who had been stealing the food from their mouths.

They were within three or four miles of Beaverton when Dancer lifted a pointing finger toward the dull shimmering glow on the horizon. Ki cursed softly.

"It's Beaverton," Jessica said. "The town's on fire."

They lifted their weary horses into a run and, with their eyes fixed on the dull glow ahead of them, raced on toward the burning town.

"The outlaws—they've struck back," Dancer said.

But it wasn't that, and Jessica knew it somehow. By the time they were within a quarter of a mile of Beaverton they could hear the sounds of shouting, of glass breaking and the occasional angry report of a weapon being fired.

Dancer was still puzzled. "What in hell could be going on?" he shouted to Jessie.

"The race war someone wanted," she shouted back tensely. "It's begun."

Chapter 10

The report had come back to Beaverton that the outlaws were Japanese, and alcohol and tough talk had fueled resentment. Beaverton had exploded suddenly with racial resentment—the Japanese feeling exploited, the whites that they were being robbed by a gang of foreigners.

"They've torched the shanty town," Ki pointed out. He was right. The shacks on the north side of town, where the Japanese miners lived, had been set afire. Now flames curled into the night sky.

Uptown someone had sought retaliation. Flames crackled and flared from near the Red Rooster Saloon and the hotel. Ki started his horse forward, but Dancer's hand fell on its bridle, halting it.

"Hold it, Ki!" Dancer shouted. "Just what in hell do you think we can do about this?"

"I don't know—all I know is that we can't do *nothing*," Ki insisted. Maybe he was right, but to Dancer things had gotten so far out of control that nobody was going to stop it or even slow it. He had seen riots before on the San Francisco docks and he knew that a mob has no mind at all. It is a brainless, many-armed beast, which prowls, seeking something to savage, wanting something to die, even if it is a part of itself.

Dancer sighed and started forward with the others. Ki refused to let Yoshiko go on, however.

"I will be beside you," she argued. "I must."

"Not here, not now. It is far too dangerous," Ki told her. Yoshiko glanced at Jessica Starbuck.

"*She* is going."

"If she wants to, yes. Jessica has seen trouble before. You have seen very little of the world. Stay here. I mean it!"

Yoshiko didn't like it at all, but she didn't dare disobey her warrior. She watched them ride off toward Beaverton, wondering what any of them, even the *te* master, could do to halt this.

"Strange situation," Dancer shouted to Jessie. "With us and Ki, no one's going to know which side we're on—they'll all be shooting at us." He was probably right, Jessie acknowledged silently. And the shooting had intensified. Someone was going to get killed, all over a foolish mistake.

"We've got to find the leaders of the mob and explain things," Jessie shouted back.

That, Ki thought, was entirely logical, but completely impractical. Who were the leaders, and was there anything that could make them stop and listen?

Entering Beaverton, they saw gangs of men running toward each other, fleeing. Rocks were thrown through windows. Now and then a gun was fired as the confused battle spread throughout the town.

As the mob grew thicker and more violent toward the center of town Ki grew more concerned for Jessica's safety.

"Dancer, take her to the hotel, will you?"

Jessie shouted an argument: "What good can I do there?"

"What good can we do anywhere?"

"What are you going to do, Ki?" Dancer asked.

"Find the marshal if I can, see just what in hell is going on."

Ki slipped from his horse's back and waved a quick farewell. There was an armed mob rushing up the street to join the fight now, and there wasn't time to stand around and see what their inclination was.

Dancer and Jessica started up the street at a trot. Three Japanese leaped out in front of them and went for the bridles of their horses. Dancer kicked one of them in the chest and sent him reeling. Then he grabbed Jessie's reins and turned both horses up an alley, riding hard for the hotel. A shadowy figure lurched into their path, and they had no time to slow down. They rode the man down, never knowing what he was after.

Ki, meanwhile, had decided to get off the main street himself. The fires still burned, although not so hotly, at both ends of town. Mobs still roamed the streets, waving ax handles, clubs, hammers, and chains.

He rounded the corner behind the general store and sprinted up the narrow dark alley toward the back of the marshal's office.

Ki never made it that far.

From a side alley three men appeared, with white bandannas around their heads. One of them had a chain, Ki saw by the dim moonlight, and the others must have been armed as well, although he saw no weapons. He did see the image drawn on their bandannas—the tiger.

"You there, wait a minute!" one of the men shouted and Ki came to a halt.

"Hell, he's Japanese," a second man said.

"Wait a minute . . ." Recognition came, and the man in the center, the one with the chain, crept nearer, head low, peering at Ki. "I know this one. He's the reason I got no teeth up front. Isn't that right, tall man?"

"I don't know what you mean," Ki said. He instinctively glanced over his shoulder. He had really walked into something here. There were two more members of the tiger gang behind him, and one of them had a shotgun.

"You know exactly what I mean," the leader of the gang said, coming nearer. "I know who you are. We've been looking for you."

"I thought you were supposed to be out stirring up trouble," Ki said. Both the comment and the relaxed tone Ki used seemed to disturb the young thug.

"Huh?"

"Keeping things brewing, destroying any chance of the Centennial working again."

"I don't know what the hell you're talking about."

"You do, but we won't argue about it," Ki replied. "Just let me go past. No need for more trouble."

"Trouble!" The thug laughed. "It's no trouble at all; as a matter of fact it's going to be a great pleasure to finish you."

He tried it with the chain before he had gotten the last words of his threat out. The chain whizzed through the air toward Ki. If it had hit his skull it would have crushed it to paste, but something went wrong.

The young thug, whose name was Koji, was grinning as he swung the chain, showing the gaps where his teeth had been. It was impossible, and Koji knew it, but the man before him turned and reached out, and before Koji could understand what had happened the chain was in Ki's hand. Ki yanked, shouldered Koji, and flipped him.

The thug landed hard on his back. The chain, still wrapped around his wrist, was going to do him no good at all now. Ki was standing on his arm, the other end of the chain in his hand.

"Now we can quit?" Ki asked in Japanese.

"Go to hell," Koji growled. He lifted his head and shouted at the others, "Kill him!"

The man with the shotgun had to hold back or spray buckshot into his own gang, but the others rushed Ki with deadly intent. The man with the knife was first. Ki took his wrist with one hand, slapped his other hand up hard beneath the elbow, and left the tiger-clan man writhing on the ground, his arm snapped at the elbow joint.

The second man took a stiffened finger in the eye, followed by a sweeping kick which took his feet from under him. He screamed and clawed at his face as he hit the ground.

The last man was wary and clever. He tried kicking at Ki's kneecap as he waved his club before him. Ki easily dodged the kick and ducked a sweep of the club past his head. Spinning, he sidekicked the thug in the ribs and then chopped at the base of his neck, paralyzing the arm which held the club.

Ki heard the shotgun click behind him and he knew he

could do nothing in time to save his own life. He flung himself to the ground, rolling, waiting for the inevitable thunderburst, the hot deadly spray of pellets.

But it didn't come.

Sitting up, Ki looked in amazement at the man with the shotgun, who had dropped his weapon and was slapping at his back for some reason. When he turned Ki saw why.

A *tonti,* a throwing knife, was imbedded in his spine. As Ki watched, the man toppled forward face first and hit the alley floor to lie there unmoving, dead.

And the Master emerged from the shadows to confront Ki.

Ki bowed from reflex and genuine respect. "Kobi-san."

"Ki," the Master said stiffly. He wore a gold robe with flaring sleeves. His white hair was knotted at the back of his narrow skull. Arched white eyebrows sheltered penetrating dark eyes.

"First you would kill me," Ki said, "and then you would save my life. Which is it you have come to do?"

"To kill you, of course," Kobi-san answered softly. He waved a hand. "But I will not have a *te* master killed by a pack of dogs such as these."

"We must speak," Ki said, taking a step toward the Master.

"No. We must fight; one must die," Kobi-san replied.

"You do not understand."

"I understand. You have stolen Yoshiko. You have prostituted your powers, selling them to a white person. You have turned your back on your own people who suffer and die here while you live well."

"This is all untrue. Listen to me for one minute—"

At the sound of running feet from behind, Ki turned his head. Three men, whites, were running toward them. The man in the lead appeared at that distance to be wearing a star.

"Kobi-san!" Ki shouted.

"No." The Master shook his head and then was gone, vanishing into an alley. "Not now..." His voice seemed to drift on the wind. "Later we shall finish this. Later one of us shall die."

The men behind Ki pounded to a stop, a few curses rising from their lips as they surveyed the carnage. One of them yanked Koji to his feet and handcuffed him.

"What is this?" Marshal King asked. As Ki turned he recognized him. "What happened here, Ki?"

Ki shrugged. "Nothing compared to what is going on out there."

"You're right there," King said, tugging at his red mustache. "It's been going on for hours. Don't know what triggered it, who hit first, but they're wrecking my town."

He glanced across his shoulder as one of his deputies roughly led Ki's attackers away.

"Don't know where we're going to put them. Jail's full; Earl Gibbons's back room we been using for a cell is full too."

A burst of gunfire and a scream of pain from the main street brought their heads around sharply.

"I got to get out there. You coming along, Ki?"

"If you want me to," Ki answered. "Your justice," he went on, "it is even-handed?"

The lawman stiffened. "If you mean am I going out there to bust Japanese heads and let the whites off easier, the answer's no. Everyone out there is breaking the law as far as I'm concerned. There's a curfew in effect, and none of them are supposed to be on the streets. If I can talk 'em home, I'll do that. If we've got to bust heads, we will— but it don't matter to me who they are."

Still, Ki had reservations, but he followed along with the posse, which had grown to half a dozen grim and determined armed men. As they walked, Ki told King briefly about the outlaw hideout and Takahashi.

"When it rains, it pours, don't it?" the marshal responded. They were hurrying through the alleys toward the heart of the trouble. "If I ever get this straightened out we'll head on over there—though it's out of my jurisdiction."

99

"Yes, I realize that. The people this is hurting are in your jurisdiction, though."

"Yeah." King's eyes lifted to the knot of men fighting in the center of the street. "When I can, Ki—you see how it is. You helping or not?"

"I am," Ki said, "helping."

Things were getting worse by the moment on Main Street. The gangs seemed to have found what they needed —leaders. The Japanese were trying to destroy white businesses in retaliation, and the whites were fighting them off.

Coming around the corner onto the street King and Ki found a half-dozen white thugs beating a Japanese, who lay on the ground, trying futilely to defend himself. If Ki had been worried about racism on Kings' part, he now lost that apprehension. King ordered his deputies to wade in and break up the beating. The deputies threw the whites aside, but when they got to the bottom of the pile, the Japanese got to his feet and sprinted away.

Ki glanced to the right and saw something that chilled him. The hotel was on fire.

"I'm leaving," he yelled to King. "The hotel. Jessica's in there."

Before King could answer, Ki was sprinting off up the street toward the hotel. He made it half the distance before three whites came out to meet him, one of them brandishing a torch like a club.

"Just hold up there, boy!" one of them yelled. But Ki had no intention of slowing. Hands grabbed for his arms as he went on past them. Ki threw an elbow into one man's nose, sending him crashing to the ground. Then he was past them, running toward the hotel, which was spewing smoke from the upstairs windows.

In the lobby Ki met pandemonium. Hotel guests, many half-dressed, were rushing toward the outer door. In the back of the lobby a gang of white thugs had encountered a knot of Japanese, and a small-scale riot was in progress. Chairs and tables were toppled and used as weapons as the manager alternately yelled at them and ducked to avoid flying objects.

Reaching the stairs, Ki found even more confusion. Smoke was beginning to roll down the stairwell and he had to fight his way through the panicked hotel guests.

He looked frantically at each face, but Jessie wasn't there; nor was Dancer. By the time he reached the landing he saw why.

Dancer had his back against the wall, his shirt ripped, his face bloody. Flames licked at the ceiling farther along the corridor. In front of Dancer four Japanese thugs stood, kicking at him, taunting. Ki recognized one of them—a tiger-gang member.

Dancer struck out with fists and feet, but it wasn't enough to drive back the gang, who carried sticks and chains.

Ki waded in.

A sidekick struck one of them in the back of the neck, and the man was smashed forward into the wall. As the second man turned, stick upraised, Ki jabbed stiffened fingers into his throat, crushing his windpipe. He settled to the floor in a heap. Ki hard the whipping sound of a chain and just managed to jerk his head back in time. The attackers had forgotten about Dancer temporarily, and that was a vital mistake.

Dancer slammed his fist into the jaw of the man with the chain, and Ki heard bone snap. The last man took off at a dead run. Dancer was sagging now and Ki helped him up.

"Where is Jessica?"

Dancer pointed toward her room and started that way, staggering. Ki heard the cry for help and easily outraced Dancer to the room where a bulky miner had Jessica pinned to the bed, her blouse ripped open. The man's head came around and his bleary eyes fixed on Ki. He tried to draw his holstered gun but Ki's kick snapped his wrist.

The miner leaped from the bed, a low growl building in his throat as he flung himself at Ki.

It wasn't the best idea the man had ever had. Ki sidestepped and tripped the man, and in the same motion he grabbed him by the seat of the pants and his shirt collar. After swinging the miner in a brief arc, Ki released him, and the miner flew through the locked window, a scream rising from his throat as he fell to the street in a shower of glass.

Ki turned sharply at the sound of approaching footsteps, but it was only Dancer, looking like a man rising from his grave. He could only pant as he spoke.

"Ki, the fire . . ." Dancer looked at Jessica, her clothing half ripped off. He snatched a blanket from the bed. "It's getting bad out there—the window?"

Ki looked that way and nodded. It was not a long jump, but long enough to break an ankle. Still, with the flames building in the corridor, it was the better option. "Go," Ki told them. "Now!"

"You . . . ?" Jessica asked.

"One minute." There was one more chore to be done. Taking a deep breath, Ki rushed out into the flaming hallway and, keeping low to avoid the bulk of the smoke, he made his way to his own room. He found the small chamois sack he was searching for, snatched it up, and scooted out of there.

Reaching the hallway again, Ki withdrew quickly. A burning timber fell from the roof of the building, scattering flame, leaving a gaping hole in the ceiling. Smoke rushed up and out the hole.

There was no way back to Jessica's room, and seconds later there would be no path to Ki's own window. He leaped the burning timber and rushed toward the staircase.

There was no one fighting there now; the flames had pushed them all out of the building, except for the single dead man sprawled on the floor. Ki hit the stairwell at a run and felt his foot drop through a charred step. Flame shot up from the gap and pain rippled through Ki's leg.

He yanked his foot out angrily and stumbled down the stairway, the banister to his right painted with flame. Below, the lobby was thick with smoke. Ki, choking, his hair singed, fought his way through to the front door and burst out into the street as another section of roof dropped into the hotel lobby.

He backed away slowly on his injured foot, watching the bright spectacle of the hotel in its flaming death throes.

"Ki!"

He turned to find Jessica, blanket around her shoulders, hair tangled, face smudged, rushing toward him. He held her for a moment, smiled, and stepped back.

"Dancer?"

"He's coming. He had to sit down for a minute. The man you tossed out the window landed on his neck."

Ki shrugged. He didn't have much sympathy for animals who tried to rape women. The street was nearly empty now. The beast had had enough, it seemed, or maybe the flames, now spreading to a nearby building, had driven them off. By the time Dancer arrived they were the only people in the street except for the hotel manager, who was standing, arms dangling, hair in his face, staring at his place of business in disbelief.

"Let's see what Marshal King can tell us," Jessica suggested.

Jessie wasn't optimistic about what was to come for Beaverton and the Centennial Mine. The breach that had existed before between white and Japanese, management and labor, had become a chasm. Reaching out with mere words wasn't going to heal things quickly.

Before they reached the marshal's office, they were intercepted by Earl Gibbons. Still pale, not looking well at all, the freight-line owner hollered at them, waving his arms.

They waited for Gibbons to catch up before Jessie asked, "What is it, Earl?"

"They hit my office, Miss Starbuck. Burned up three wagons, too."

"We'll replace them, I promise you."

"By tomorrow?" Gibbons asked, struggling to keep the deep emotion out of his voice.

"Why tomorrow? What do you mean?"

"I saw Strangfeld. He's got a load of silver ingots ready to go."

"Now? Impossible! We just shipped a load out."

"Yes," Gibbons panted, "but apparently he was holding at least half of what was available back because of the outlaws. Ki's plan got that lot through and he was ready to go again; they wouldn't expect it so soon. Now, with the mine apparently closed down, with thugs running the town, he decided to go immediately. I'm the only one he told—you two were gone—but someone heard somehow and burned my wagons."

It was difficult not to feel sorry for Gibbons: shot, harassed, burned out. It was equally difficult not to be angry with Strangfeld for not saying he was holding back on the shipment. But then again, who knew who to trust anymore in Beaverton?

"I wonder if the stable was attacked," Ki said as they approached the marshal's office. "There could be wagons there still."

"Maybe—that's our last hope, isn't it? I mean, we're not carrying the goods to the capital."

"Just keep quiet about this," Jessica said to Gibbons, who looked hurt by the suggestion that he had a loose tongue. "We'll get it straightened around."

Quietly, Jessica and Ki discussed matters. "I have to think Strangfeld is right—get the silver out of here and fast," Ki said.

"It's set now. We'll go with his plan. He is still the mine manager," Jessica answered.

They broke off the discussion as they reached King's office. It was a crowded mess inside. Blood spattered the floor. Two bruised deputies glanced up unhappily. King looked a question at Gibbons, who shook his head in answer. From the back of the jail they heard men cursing and yelling in two languages until King ordered the door closed.

"You and Fred go on home now," King said to one of his tired men. "I'll come get you if this thing erupts again."

The deputy gave the marshal a pained look and started toward the door. In another minute, Jessie, Ki, Dancer, and Gibbons were alone with the lawman, who had poured himself a whisky.

"I still don't know what happened," he said. "All of a sudden men were bashing each other and destroying the town. Someone said the Japs were behind the robberies. That true?"

"Only partly," Ki answered. He went on to give King a fuller explanation of what he and Jessie had discovered.

"Terrific—any guesses as to who's behind it all?" King asked, turning his glass slowly.

"No good ones. Do your own speculating. Do you know Strangfeld is making another shipment tomorrow?"

"Yeah, he told me." The marshal finished off his drink. "That's all I need. Think I'll find me another line of work."

"We'll be going along," Jessica said. "Unless you're going to go after the outlaws at Castle Wells."

"Are you kidding? With who for a posse? I couldn't round up three men with the way things are."

"Well then, we'll try to help get the silver through—if we can find any wagons."

"Good luck," King said numbly. "Oh, yeah, the other thing . . ."

"What other thing?" Ki asked.

"The girl—that girl you were looking for."

Ki's eyes narrowed. "We've already found her." Marshal King's own face mirrored Ki's confusion.

"Did you?" he asked. "Couple of my men came across her outside of town—girl named Yoshiko. Said she wanted to catch up with a man called Ki. Deputies started bringing her in to me."

"And?" Ki asked feeling his pulse rate begin to lift.

"And," King shrugged, "they got hit. You know how things were—a couple of Japanese snatched her and took her off. Where, God only knows."

★

Chapter 11

In four days in Beaverton Jessie and Ki hadn't accomplished a damn thing. In fact things were worse than when they had come to town. Over breakfast Jessica counted off their problems.

"The mine's closed indefinitely. The outlaws run things outside of the town limits; the mobs inside. Gibbons's business is staggering. Yoshiko is gone again—who knows where."

"Yes, not exactly a successful expedition so far." Ki sipped at his tea and shook his head. "You forgot to mention Kobi-san, who presumably is still waiting for his chance to kill me, and the fact that we have no idea who is behind all this." He unconsciously patted his vest pockets where the throwing stars, rescued at the last minute from the hotel fire, rested. Touching them gave him no sense of security at all. What use were weapons without targets?

"Earl Gibbons has two wagons. Not the best, but they'll do," Jessie said. "Hired from a ranch. Old hay wagons. They've got the bulk to do the job."

"All right." Ki was pragmatic on this cool Colorado morning. "Let's see what we can do about making sure this shipment gets through safely. The other problems seem to have us buffaloed for now."

"The outlaws will already know the shipment is going out," Jessica commented.

"Yes. They will." Whoever was tipping the outlaws was very likely still on top of things. There was no use hoping that they could slip out of Beaverton unseen. Still, Ki thought, there were a few precautions they could take. "We are going to have to change Strangfeld's plans just a little bit. The shipping time, for one thing."

"It's varied, as always." Jessica dabbed at her mouth with a napkin, folded it, and put it aside. Half of her breakfast was still on her plate. The situation wasn't conducive to appetite.

"I was thinking of something different—trying it at night," Ki told her.

"The worst time, isn't it? It gives the outlaws cover."

"And us, maybe. Going out in broad daylight hasn't kept them from trying a raid."

"How about the marshal? Is King going to do anything to help us out this time?"

"What can he do?" Ki asked. "The trouble in town is liable to erupt at any time. The few deputies he could round up are at the mine to prevent trouble there, or are roaming the streets."

"Ki—someone has to talk to the miners, all of them." Jessie's sea-green eyes were concerned, serious. "Someone's got them working against each other until they all stand to lose their livelihoods."

"And the Centennial goes bust because of it."

"Yes, and someone other than Starbuck Enterprises moves in to take over the mine. That's the grand plan, isn't it, Ki?"

"So it seems. And if it is, Jessica, someone has already made a good start on bringing it about."

Dancer sauntered into the restaurant, limping slightly, still a little gray in the face, bruised and weary. He walked to where they sat and sagged into a chair, refusing even coffee.

"What's up?" he asked.

"Just trying to work out a few things—not that we've had much luck doing that so far. Ki has an idea for timing the silver shipment. I'm trying to figure out a way of communicating with the miners, of slowing things down."

"You're the mine owner," Dancer said. "If they won't listen to you, who will they listen to?"

"Maybe no one. I was thinking . . ."

The restaurant door opened again and they saw a tired looking Marshal King walking toward their table. He had his hand resting on the butt of his holstered Colt, and despite his apparent weariness there was caution and purpose in King's expression. He stopped just before the table, behind Ki, and said:

"Dancer. Keep your hands on the table. I'm taking you in."

"For what?" Dancer laughed.

"There's nothing funny about this." King glanced at Jessica. "If you and Ki don't have anything to do with this, keep your own hands still, Miss Starbuck."

"To do with what?" Jessica asked. "What's Dancer supposed to have done?"

"He's done a murder," King said, drawing his Colt smoothly and slowly, hooking the hammer back with his thumb before he stepped behind Dancer and disarmed him.

"Murder?" Dancer's hands went up automatically. He gave Jessica a puzzled look and shook his head. "I'm afraid I don't know what you're talking about, Marshal."

"Maybe not," King said, shoving Dancer's gun behind his belt, stepping back a little. "We'll find out. Why don't you get to your feet now, Dancer? Slowly, if you will."

Dancer pushed back his chair but didn't rise immediately. "Mind telling me who I'm supposed to have killed?"

"A man named Jack Troupe was found covered over with a few pine branches back up in the hills. Your wallet was there in the grave, Dancer."

Dancer looked again at Jessica. Watching her eyes he said, "I didn't kill him. The idea's ridiculous."

"Maybe. I ain't judge or jury. All I know is when I find a man's identification beside a dead body I've got probable cause to arrest him, and that's what I'm doing."

"Dancer and Troupe worked together," Jessica said. "We can wire San Francisco and establish that."

"Could if we had any telegraph wires up," the marshal responded. "After last night's rampage, we don't. Besides, that don't prove nothing, does it, Miss Starbuck? Sorry. I

108

know Dancer's your friend, but he's the best—only—suspect I got in this case, and he's going along with me."

"I didn't do it, Jessica. I'm who I told you I am," Dancer said, getting to his feet as heads in the restaurant turned toward them to see what was going on.

"I believe you, Michael," she said. She didn't have a chance to say anything else before the marshal turned him and walked him toward the door, where an armed deputy waited.

Ki watched the men's backs until they were gone. Then he returned to his tea. Jessica was watching him closely.

"You're still not sure of Michael Dancer, are you?"

"Are you?" Ki was silent for a minute. "The telegraph line concerns me. It cuts us off from any outside help, and outside help appears to be what we'll need to break the outlaw gang up."

"It doesn't get easier, does it, Ki?" Jessie asked. She pushed her tray away and called for the waitress, obviously upset.

Outside, it was clear and cold. The air still smelled of smoke and ash. The hotel was a dismal pile of charred timber. They stood for a minute, staring silently; then Jessica sucked in a deep breath and said, "All right, we've got things to do."

"The miners?"

"I think that's first. There's got to be some way to get everyone together to talk this over before the town is destroyed and the streets littered with the dead."

"You think talking will do any good?"

"I think I have to try. I owe that much to the innocent people caught up in this. I'll talk with Strangfeld first, tell him about the shipment, and see if he can't introduce me to some of the leaders among the miners."

"What do you want me to do?" Ki asked.

"I thought that was a foregone conclusion," Jessica answered. Ki nodded. It was indeed.

He was going to find Yoshiko.

He worked first on who might have taken her—assuming the report they had gotten was true, as it seemed to be.

She had followed them to town after all and gotten herself carried off. The tiger gang? Likely. They seemed to be working for Takahashi and whoever he worked for. But why snatch Yoshiko again?

Ki thought he knew, but it was just speculation. He got a horse from the stable, a big buckskin with a black mane and tail, and rode slowly out of town, still speculating.

It all came back to Kobi-san.

If someone wanted to snare Ki or Kobi-san, he needed to have Yoshiko for bait. All the better if Kobi-san could be convinced that Ki was behind the kidnapping.

Ki turned it over in his mind carefully, and it seemed to make sense in one way: Dancer was in jail, probably framed for murder. If Ki too was out of the way, ambushed or forced to fight the Master, that left Jessica alone against the outlaws and the town's chaos. A chill passed through Ki as he realized the next step would be to eliminate Jessica. They'd already tried that and would again. With that done, the outlaws would have no one to oppose them. Probably Jack Troupe was killed out of the same motive.

Ki felt the wind in his face, a cold, steady wind which lifted his horse's mane. Glancing northward, he decided it would rain soon, and hard. Before that happened he wanted to find Yoshiko's tracks and try following them to wherever she was being held.

At the little knoll where they had left Yoshiko the night before, Ki swung down and searched back and forth. There were signs of impatience there, much pacing back and forth, an occasional tiny hollow where Yoshiko had kicked at the earth in disgust.

Ki could imagine it all too clearly. The girl standing there, watching the town burn, finally deciding to mount and ride into Beaverton herself.

He swung aboard the buckskin again and rode westward, angling toward the north end of town, the Japanese end, following Yoshiko's little horse's tracks.

Ki's expression was one of puzzlement. Yoshiko, he assumed, had tried to follow him into Beaverton and somehow been kidnapped there; but she was riding in the wrong direction.

All right, then; she had another purpose in mind.

Maybe, growing cold and bored, worried about friends in the shantytown, she had decided to go home, despite the fires and fighting.

Or she had gone to find Kobi-san, to try to talk to him. That, on inspection, seemed to be a logical alternative, knowing Yoshiko. But something had gone wrong somewhere.

Ki lost the tracks at the edge of the shantytown, and he drew up with a sigh, staring at the houses. A few of them were destroyed by fire; others were covered with ash. He had no wish to enter the town again; it was a foreign country, off-limits to the half-American Ki, who was so closely identified with the mine's owner.

There was little choice. He went on down, leading the horse, as a soft, cold rain began to fall from the Colorado skies.

The deputy hadn't mentioned where Yoshiko had been kidnapped. In fact, he didn't say how he knew about it. King hadn't bothered to ask more questions, at least not in Ki's presence, but then the marshal had had a lot on his mind just then.

All Ki could do was go from house to house once more, knowing that the tiger gang would be watching, waiting for another chance to even up the score. As would Kobi-san.

He went first to the house of the old woman who had talked to him, but her male relatives, home from the mines now, refused to let Ki in.

"Just a simple question or two," Ki said in Japanese.

The squat, hard-faced man facing him refused to budge an inch. "No, no questions. Go away."

Someone behind the miner muttered, "American bastard child."

Ki tensed slightly, but he had heard such slurs from childhood. He simply repeated his words. "I only want to ask a question. About the woman, Yoshiko."

"We don't know her. We don't talk to the dogs of the American mine owner."

"Don't talk to me then," Ki said, a touch of anger for the first time creeping into his voice. "But do something for your people—talk to the American woman. Didn't she see that you got the same wages as the Americans? Hasn't she seen that your people no longer have all the hazardous jobs?"

The man tensed and seemed ready to fly at Ki's throat. "Nothing has changed, nothing! We do the same jobs. Do you want me to show you my pay for a month's work? All that has changed is that the Americans have come down here and set fire to our homes."

"Strangfeld was supposed to see to it," Ki said. Now he was concerned. Strangfeld, it seemed, had deliberately disobeyed Jessica's directives, and perhaps that alone had triggered of the riots. The whites, already primed by the knowledge that some Japanese, the tiger gang, were involved in the robberies, had swarmed down to the shantytown and burned it.

"Go away now, go away," the little man said, shoving Ki in the chest. It was a very dangerous thing to do, but the *te* master understood frustration and anger. He had no wish to strike back. Ki simply bowed and tried again to explain things.

"If you would talk to Jessica Starbuck, you and your leaders—" he began, but the door to the shanty was slammed in his face, and Ki was left alone in the cold rain to stare at it.

He spotted the boy out of the corner of his eye and only slowly did it register. That was the one who had come to him with the Castle Wells message.

Ki called out after the child, but the boy vanished around the corner of an alley. Ki started that way at a trot. Around another corner he had a brief glimpse of the boy. The alley was strangled with used barrels and refuse but Ki squeezed through and continued on, calling out again.

"Hey, boy!"

Those were the last words he said for a long time. He

just saw the arc of an object whipping toward his head. Then he felt a stunning blow on the base of his skull, and he pitched forward against the cold, muddy earth of the alley floor, as the rain fell down.

Jessica stood in front of the door to Mike Strangfeld's office, blocking his exit. Strangfeld looked like he wanted to flee the office, get away from this crazy blonde once and for all.

"I saw the books," Jessica told him again. "The Japanese are still making less than the whites. I suppose there's some explanation for that, but there's none that's going to stand up, Strangfeld."

"It seemed easier all around to start at the first of the month," Strangfeld answered.

"Easier for who? Not for the Japanese, certainly," Jessie said. Strangfeld was hunched forward, his big fists clenching and unclenching. The man wasn't used to being talked to like this, not by a slip of a woman.

"For the bookkeepers, for the payroll clerk, for everybody," Strangfeld said bitterly. "Look, I'm still running this outfit. I made a decision; maybe it was the wrong one, but it seemed like it was for the best at the time."

"Did it? Did you see the town last night, Strangfeld? You don't suppose this policy of yours had anything to do with that, do you—with building up the resentment of the Japanese?"

"It didn't have anything to do with them robbing my silver shipments!" Strangfeld roared. "Look, I said it before: If you want me to quit, Miss Starbuck, I will. Step away from the door and I'll be on my way. You think you can find someone else to honcho this outfit, you go look for him."

"I don't want you to quit," Jessie said with exasperation. "What I want is for you to run Centennial the way it's intended to be run—fairly and honestly."

Strangfeld didn't like the last word at all. "Are you saying that I'm doing something dishonest up here, Miss Starbuck? Because if you are, you don't have to give my resigning a second thought. I'm gone."

"That's not what I meant," Jessie said somewhat soothingly. "I was just trying to make a point. There's a way to operate a business and a way not to. The first thing a man in your position might want to consider is who's paying his wages and who is giving the orders. You might also consider that I'd probably have an easier time finding a new mine manager right on the premises than you'd have of finding a new job at your wages."

"Maybe," Strangfeld said, resignation creeping into his tone. "I'll see that it's done anyway. Not that it matters much right now. I had six men show up for work this morning."

"Six!"

"That's right. Everybody's afraid of trouble breaking out up here, it seems. Tell you the truth, I was scared of it too. That's exactly what would happen. The men who showed up—well, there's Max, my bookkeeper, and the boys in the shipping department. No one wants to go down in the shaft when the man behind him's got a shovel or pickax."

"We'll get this straightened around," Jessie said. "The first thing I want is to talk to your foremen, or any others who have an influence on the miners."

The suspicion was back in Strangfeld's eyes. "What for, lady? You got some crazy idea of bringing the boys back?"

"That's what we're here for, isn't it? Both of us. Yes, that's the idea. Then if we get some of the Japanese leaders to listen to us . . ."

"Never work," Strangfeld blurted out. "The boys know the Japanese are behind the robberies. They know who burned part of the town last night."

"I don't think anyone knows who is behind the robberies, Strangfeld. I can tell you this—they're not all Japanese; nor are all of the Japanese involved. Most of them want to get back to work, nothing more. Isn't that what the others want?"

"Well." He scratched his jaw. "Yes. But it won't—"

"We don't know what will work until we try it. There won't be time to organize a meeting today; we'll be too busy getting the next silver shipment out. But I want you to talk to the leaders later tonight."

"All right," Strangfeld grumbled. "Whatever you say, boss." The last word was heavy with sarcasm, but Jessie let it pass without comment. Let Strangfeld have his small victories.

"Earl Gibbons should have those hay wagons by now, axles greased, equipment checked out. We still have our horses—or did the mob run them off too?"

"We got 'em. I set a guard on 'em when the trouble started," Strangfeld told her. "I'll take care of that, don't worry. When we pull out in the morning—"

"That was the other thing," Jessica Starbuck said as Strangfeld turned toward the coatrack, where his hat hung. He stopped, hand poised in the air.

"What was the other thing?" he asked. There was pain in his dark eyes.

"We're not leaving in the morning. We're pulling out tonight about midnight. See that everything's ready by then."

Chapter 12

Damn it all, now what?

Jessica Starbuck, wearing a short plaid mackinaw, stood watching the silver being loaded onto the wagons by torchlight. It was raining still, and very cold as the wind increased. She wore gloves and hat, but still her hands were half frozen. From time to time she shifted the Winchester rifle she was carrying from hand to hand. At each footstep she turned to look toward the main gate of the mine, but he wasn't there.

Where in hell was Ki?

He hadn't been at the hotel or at the restaurant. He knew the plan, knew they were pulling out at midnight. He wouldn't have pulled a vanishing act at this point unless it was for something vital and urgent.

Or unless he had had no choice.

Jessie had dropped by the marshal's office and talked to Dancer. She had had a look at the evidence the marshal had, and lost an argument to grant Dancer bail.

"If he did a murder he's not getting out of here for all the money in the Starbuck empire," King had said.

"He *didn't* do it."

King shook his head. "The evidence says there's every chance he might have, Miss Starbuck. I'm doing my job, and you know it. I'd likely lose my badge if I turned him loose."

"I need him for tonight," Jessica pleaded.

"Sorry about that. Think about it though—he might be just the man you don't want along tonight. Strangfeld is going to send three extra men, and Gibbons is sending the usual guards. Jack Taylor's going to ride shotgun. If that ain't enough, Dancer here isn't going to be enough either."

After relinquishing her Colt, Jessie was allowed to see Dancer. He was clenching the bars of his cell door tightly, his eyes flashing. Jessie placed one of her hands over his.

"We'll work this out, Michael. I promise you."

"Will we?" Dancer was uncharacteristically gloomy. The smile was gone. "Someone's done a job on me, Jessie. And if they don't hang me, someone's going to be disappointed enough to finish me off in jail."

King heard that and swiveled around in his chair. "I don't like that talk, Dancer. No one's going to lynch a prisoner of mine, and as little as I can spare a man, I'll have an extra deputy posted in the alley behind the jail."

"Has Ki been in?" Jessica asked Dancer.

"Ki? No. Was he going to come over?"

"I don't know. He's disappeared on me."

"He'll show up tonight. Maybe he's found Yoshiko."

King was at the window looking out, hands behind his back, as Jessie gave Dancer a brief, torrid kiss. She smiled. "We'll get you out of here."

King turned slowly toward Jessica as she walked to his desk and picked up her gun. She tossed back her hair, set her hat, and walked to him.

"How does everything look on the streets?" she asked.

"It's early still," King said glumly. "Wait until full dark; wait until they've had a few drinks . . . There's nothing to be real optimistic about, except that the rain's still falling. That'll keep some of 'em home, cut down on the arson."

King looked tired, and it was no wonder. He was sitting on a smoldering powder keg, and the town expected him to keep the lid on it. "Let's hope that meeting of yours comes off, Miss Starbuck. And hope it does some good. These men aren't much in the mood for listening."

"They'll listen," Jessica said. "They'll have to listen." It was only wishful thinking and both of them knew it; still, she had to believe it. She went out into the rain and walked the streets for a while, looking for Ki, but couldn't find him anywhere.

117

By midnight he still hadn't shown.

"How long are we going to wait for him?" Jack Taylor asked.

"You're not loaded yet."

"We will be any minute," the freight foreman said. "After that, any time we spend hanging around here is asking for trouble. If this is going to work, we'd better get gone once we're loaded."

Jessie thought for a moment, glancing at the wagons and then again at the gate. "You're right, Jack. As soon as the silver's on board, we'll pull out."

Looking relieved, Taylor walked away toward the loading dock. Ki just wasn't going to make it, Jessica decided. Well, all she could do was hope that it was good luck at finding Yoshiko that kept him away.

Jessie swung herself onto the back of the pert little paint pony she was riding and sat watching the last tarp being tied down. Strangfeld stood gloomily in the rain, staring at Jessie. At last he walked to her horse and, with his hand on the pony's neck, said, "This had better work, Miss Starbuck. You know what that trail's going to be like in the dark and rain? We might not need to worry about the outlaws at all; it'll take luck to get through at all."

Strangfeld was right. The rain was starting to pour down. It was too late to second-guess themselves now, however. "We'll make it through," she answered.

"Sure." Strangfeld pulled his collar up. "I'll tell you what. I'm glad I'm not going. The miners I talked to don't like much about having that meeting, by the way. But I convinced 'em it's come or forget about working for Centennial. We'll be waiting at the town hall at seven o'clock tomorrow night." He looked skyward again. "Assuming you make it back to be there."

Then Strangfeld patted the paint horse's damp neck, pocketed his hands, and trudged away heavily toward his office, where the bookkeeper was still working and smoke rose into the rainy night from a crooked black iron pipe.

"We ready?" Jack Taylor called from the loading dock. Jessie lifted a hand.

"Ready!" Or as ready as they were going to get. Glancing once more toward the main gate, Jessica started her pony, falling in behind the silver-bearing wagon and its outriders. It was going to be a long, cold night, and possibly a bloody one. She wished Ki were there again, and then gave up the wishful thinking.

They rode out of the gate and down the long muddy road toward Beaverton, which seemed fairly peaceful just now, although earlier they had heard two shots from the south end of town. Maybe only someone celebrating. Maybe a dead man for Marshal King to worry about.

They took the cutoff road behind the town and Jessica had only a feeble glimpse of the lighted window at the back of the jailhouse—enough of a glimpse to show her the dark silhouette of a man leaning against the bars, peering out.

The rain fell down and the wind gusted bansheelike in the pines beside the road. No one spoke. There was nothing to say, and no one could have been heard over five feet away. For mile after mile they rode in silence, Jessie hearing only the drumming of the cold rain on her hat. The wagons sloughed around from time to time. The horses were working hard at it. Jessica watched the darkness around them, trying to detect trouble before it came, but she could see no more than fifteen yards or so.

They crossed a tiny quick-running creek and bogged down. Jack Taylor leaped from the wagon, cursing and screaming. *Him* they could hear above the crash of the rain.

"I knew it, goddamn it! Knew the son-of-a-bitchin' horses couldn't pull this load on this road. Get that other team off the second wagon, Harry."

Harry balked. "Jesus, Jack, that's a lot of trouble."

"Get the team unhitched or I'll hitch *you* to it, damn you," Jack Taylor roared. He was like a man possessed. It made no sense until Jessica realized the man was scared half to death—scared of getting hit again. He'd survived four robberies, and maybe he didn't figure his luck could last forever.

It was a bad place to be stuck, all right; down in the narrow gully with no place to run, no place to hide. Jessica rode her pony down the bank and up the creek toward Taylor.

"Anything I can do?" she called out.

"Yeah, stay out of the way!" Taylor shouted back, his temper flashing again.

Jessica backed her pony and urged it to scrabble up the far bank. Below, the men, occasionally lighted by flashing lightning, worked like dark, rain-glossed demons.

Jessica rode a slow circle around the outskirts, finding nothing, seeing no one. By the time she got back, both wagons were up on the far side of the gully and rolling on southward.

"Holy shit!" A guard, jumpy like the rest of them, brought his gun up as Jessica rode in. Shakily he lowered his weapon as he figured out who it was. "Christ, lady, don't do that again, all right?"

"Sorry. I should've known better," Jessica answered, and that was the truth. She had seen men killed in camps in Indian country when they rode in without announcing themselves.

Jack Taylor, riding in the bed of the second wagon, yelled back, "What's happening there, Collins?"

"Nothing! I almost shot the boss, that's all."

Taylor didn't answer. The way things were going he probably didn't think it criminal to shoot the lady who had dragged them out into a night like this one.

"At least they haven't hit us yet," Jessica said out loud, No one heard her, so she rode on in silence.

There was no warning when the accident occurred. The front wagon was rolling along fine one minute and then, with a violent snapping sound, it was sitting sprawled on the muddy road, the wheels splayed out, the rear axle broken.

Jack Taylor was a madman leaping from the back of the wagon to inspect things. "Damn broken-down hay wagons!

I knew they'd never take the load. Told Gibbons a dozen times."

He shouted at one of the men who had gathered around him in the darkness. "Wheeler, this is your job. Get it rolling."

Wheeler laughed without meaning to. "Get it rolling! How in hell am I supposed to do that?"

"You're the carpenter."

"Right, sure I am, Jack. But I'm not a magician and I'm not an owl. Maybe come daylight we can do something if we can find a good tree around here. I can't patch it together with spit."

Taylor was fuming, but the other man was right. Whatever needed to be done wasn't going to be done in near pitch-darkness in the middle of a muddy road. Taylor looked around helplessly for a moment before he decided.

"All right. Get the other wagon off the road. Not far— the little knoll."

"Then what, Jack?"

"Might as well unhitch 'em and crawl under the tarps— that's where we're going to be sleeping, it looks like." He looked at Jessie as if it were all her fault, and asked sarcastically, "All right?"

"Doesn't seem we have much choice," Jessica shouted back above the rain. Taylor didn't acknowledge that he had heard her.

The wagon was drawn up onto a knoll twenty yards from the road. Two men were sent to sleep under the tarp of the broken wagon; two others were assigned to stand watch.

"Now," Taylor grumbled, "I just need to find a place for the lady to sleep."

"I've got a groundsheet and a blanket," Jessica said. "Under the wagon is good enough for me." Taylor gave her a look as if he wished she were under the broken wagon. Then he stalked away, yelling at anyone who was near enough.

Jessica rolled out her bed under the wagon, not figuring she was going to sleep much that night anyway. It was miserably cold and damp, and she had too many things to worry about—far too many.

She couldn't remember a job she and Ki had taken on that had gotten so snarled on itself. They didn't seem to be making progress on any front. More problems simply cropped up.

Instead of just Yoshiko being missing, now Ki was gone as well—or Kobi-san had . . . No, she wouldn't think of that possibility. Dancer was locked up in Beaverton's jail, and whether they could make that murder charge stick or not he was of no help at all just now. Nothing had been done about the tense racial situation, and the Centennial wasn't even operating just now.

Jessie lay and watched the rain, tugging her blanket up over her ears. Now and then she saw a sentry walk by. From time to time thunder boomed and lightning flashed. It was one of the worst nights of her life and certainly one of the most uncomfortable.

The only way to escape the discomfort seemed to be to try sleeping. Maybe she wouldn't feel the cold then and she wouldn't have to keep on with that fruitless worrying. Jessica wrapped her blanket around her even more tightly and, surprisingly, did sleep, although her dreams were unsettling and bloody.

She awoke when the thunder roared and a man cried out in anguished pain. Awakening was much more bloody than the twisted dreams. Jessie reached for her rifle.

Beyond the wagon a dozen riders stormed toward them, guns flashing in the rainy night. She saw one of Gibbons's guards go down in the mud. Then one of the raiders toppled backward from his horse.

Jessica sighted one man, triggered off, and saw her shot miss. The second time she blew away half of his right arm and switched her sights to a second target.

The Winchester malfunctioned and Jessica breathed a curse. The battle raged around her while she tried to unjam it. Above her, Jack Taylor's shotgun roared and another raider was down.

It was suddenly silent. Jessica slowly cocked her rifle

and watched from under the wagon as men in slickers approached her.

"That's all of 'em, I guess. Look under the tarp."

Someone clambered aboard and threw the tarp aside. "It's here. Thousands."

"The boss knew. Think his tip was bad?"

"Never thought they'd try it at this time of night."

Someone called from below, "What about the other wagon, Duke?"

"Hell, leave it. What else can we do? Tommy'll drive this one. Get that team up here."

Jessica held her breath as the man leaped down from the wagon, spurs clinking, and walked to the box. He was so near she could have reached out and touched him.

Half a dozen riders approached them, circling the wagon as the team was backed. She could hear the trace chains as they were hooked. Twisting her head around, she watched the feet of the men hitching the horses to the hay wagon.

Damn it all. Her breath was coming in tight little puffs. Her heart was incredibly loud, pounding away in her ears. Just what was going to happen when they drove the silver-laden wagon off? Easy. Someone was going to spot her and finish her off.

She looked up at the undercarriage of the wagon, wondering. It was a poor idea, but what choice was there? Maybe down the road there would be a chance to drop unseen from beneath the wagon.

She didn't have long to think it over.

"Let's roll it," someone shouted, and Jessie, gripping a cross-member, hooking her feet over the rear axle, hung on for dear life as the wagon, surrounded by its outlaw contingent, jolted off down the road.

Chapter 13

It took Ki a long while to shake off the clouds inside his skull and sit up, trying to remember what had happened. The boy. Yes, that was it, the boy had led him neatly into a trap, and someone had tried to crush his skull for him with a very heavy object.

Ki was sitting on a cold stone floor. There was only a ribbon of light bleeding through a high window into the building, which he couldn't identify immediately.

The boy. Well, he had fallen for it twice. The odds were pretty damn good that the message about Castle Wells had been a trap as well—a trick to draw Ki to the outlaws' haven. It sure seemed, looking back, that he and Jessica had been expected at Takahashi's house.

Ki shook his aching head and tried to get to his feet, finding out that he couldn't. His legs had been secured with a chain around the ankles and a few frantic minutes spent trying to free them were futile.

Where in hell was he? He looked around at the deeply shadowed room. A storeroom of some sort, but where? Outside, there was a muffled creaking and the sound of water running. Somewhere close to a river.

Before his thinking could carry him any further the door banged open and two armed men entered. Ki knew both of them. They were Marshal King's deputies.

"I should have known," Ki said.

"Slow, ain't you?" the man named Fred said with a crooked grin. He walked to Ki and for the hell of it kicked him hard in the ribs, sending the samurai sprawling. It felt like a rib had cracked, and the hammering in Ki's skull had begun again even more heavily, but there was one satisfaction in the attack. The muffled jangle in his pockets told Ki that they had not found or taken the throwing stars concealed there.

He sat up slowly, peering at the deputies, who were plainly pleased with themselves, and ready to inflict more pain. Ki felt like kicking himself. He should have known that it was King who was behind it all. King, who knew every move that Gibbons planned, every idea Jessie and Ki came up with.

He thought back to the night of the riot, when King and his men had been so diligent in yanking white miners off the Japanese who had fled. Of course they had—the man on the ground had been one of their own, a tiger-clan man.

"Where's King?" Ki asked.

"You don't need to know, but I expect he'll be along. He had another job in town."

"Starting fires?"

"I told you this Jap ain't dumb," Fred said.

"Just a little too slow."

"Where's the girl?" Ki asked. "Where's Yoshiko?"

"That don't matter to you," Fred said.

"I just wanted to know if she is safe." Ki's eyes were intent. He was measuring the men, watching the angles of their weapons, trying to gauge their readiness as one of his hands lifted slowly toward his vest.

"She's plenty safe. Nothing's going to happen to her for a while. Not until the old man's out of our hair."

"Kobi-san?"

"Yeah, that one. King knows something about the Japanese. He knows the old man's some kind of priest, and that if he ever got to talking to the miners, they'd listen."

That was true. The Master was a priest in Japan, and the people did not forget the old ways after a few years in a new country. They would listen to Kobi-san as if they had come to the monastery for his advice.

"They listened to him about me, didn't they?" Ki said almost to himself. Of course no one in the Japanese com-

125

munity would talk to him. They had heard Kobi-san, who was convinced that Ki had stolen Yoshiko.

"The girl," Fred said, "stays alive as long as the old man does. We'll catch up with him, though. The old man's like a ghost, but we'll find him—like we found you."

"Don't you worry about the girl," the other deputy said. "She'll be fed and clothed, and probably bedded." A dirty little laugh followed that and Ki felt his stomach tighten.

"Jessica Starbuck . . . ?"

"She'll be found too."

That meant that Jessie was still alive as far as these men knew. Ki let out a slow breath. Through the open door he could see now what sort of building he had been brought to. A huge millstone sat at rest below and beyond him. The room where he had been locked was the granary for the old mill.

"Let's finish this and get out of here," the deputy said with nervousness creeping into his voice.

Fred had better nerves. "We will. Not here, though. Outside—a bullet in the head and into the river."

Ki's eyes showed no emotion as the deputy bent to unlock the chain around Ki's ankles, but emotion was surging through him. They were giving him his chance, his one chance.

The deputy was bent over Ki's foot as the chain fell free. Ki's slippered foot sliced upward, ripping into the man's throat. Before Fred could step around his comrade and squeeze off a shot, a *shuriken* had found its way into Ki's capable fingers. It sliced, whirring, into the outlaw's face.

Fred fell back, the throwing star protruding from his eye. The rifle discharged into the stone floor, ricocheting wildly around the room. Ki was on his feet, finishing the man in front of him with a short chop to the neck. Fred needed no finishing. The *shuriken*'s blade had touched gray matter, stopping the brain's functions. The man, still on his feet, was already dead.

Ki kicked the rifle aside and started for the door. Outside, a narrow open loft ran around three sides of the old stone building to the stairs on either end of the U.

"Ki! Stop; I challenge you."

Ki froze and looked downward, one hand on the rail. There, beside the great millstone, was the Master. In his hand was a *shuriken*.

"I will not fight you!" Ki hollered back, his voice echoing through the long-dead mill.

"Give me Yoshiko."

"I do not have her. Come with me! Together we shall look for her."

"You are a traitor to your vows, Ki!" The tiny man in the white robe took a few steps forward, his sandaled feet silent against the chaff on the stone mill-floor. He lifted his eyes to the loft where Ki stood.

"I am a traitor to nothing, to no one," Ki answered.

"You tempted Yoshiko to this pagan land. You stole her away."

"No, I did not steal her away," Ki said. A bird fluttered at the window behind him and his eyes darted that way. The Master was now nearer yet, the *shuriken* still resting softly in his palm.

"You violated her body, Ki; this I know."

Ki didn't answer. His mouth tightened. He was looking at a death he could not fight against. There was nothing that could make him kill his old teacher, nothing.

"You do not answer me, Ki. Then you did lie down with her. I know this."

"What is wrong with a man and a woman giving comfort, Master Kobi-san? Where does it say that this is a wrong thing to do?"

"She was to be prioress of the monastery, Ki! A holy woman, a virgin untouched!"

"I did not know," Ki said quietly. Then, measuring his words carefully, he added, "She did not choose that, Kobi-san. It was not what she wanted. Why should you bend her will to what she does not wish?"

"That is a Western thought, Ki. That is the way of this pagan country, perhaps, but it is not ours, and you know it full well—you who studied at the monastery, you who learned *te* there, you who shared our rice, although you were Western, and filled with the disorder of Western thoughts."

The Master's voice trembled. Ki knew there was no way he was going to reach the old man with his arguments. He had lived too long with the old ways, too long with the dream of keeping Yoshiko with him at the monastery, of keeping her prisoner to a life she did not want.

"Come down, Ki. Come down and fight, or die where you stand."

Any other man would have been dead seconds later, anyone without Ki's reflexes, without his knowledge of what was to come. The throwing star the Master sent his way was only a silver blur in the eye's perception, but Ki had been expecting it, and he recognized the tiny, shoveling motion of the Master's hand for what it was.

Half turning, Ki leaped for the window behind him, his shoulder breaking through the old wood of the frame as the *shuriken* sang off the stone where his head had been a split second ago.

Ki heard the strange, ululating cry of frustration rise from the Master's lips. Then he heard nothing. Below him was the mill wheel and the river. The mill wheel was within inches of his body as he fell past it, relaxing his body, not tensing it, as he slammed into the icy face of the river and was swept away by the quick, cold current.

Gasping for breath, Ki surfaced and looked back in time to see the figure of a man at the dimly lighted window. Then he was around a bend in the river, being swept along through the trees by the water, which had begun to froth and tumble.

Stroking toward ashore, Ki dragged himself up onto the muddy bank to lie beneath the cottonwood trees, shivering as rain fell down from out of the night sky. His breathing was deep, ragged. Each breath was like filling his lungs with jagged, icy glass.

The rib they had broken was like a lance in the side, and his head still ached as if they had taken sledgehammers to it. Still, there was no time to lie there and recover, and Ki rolled to his hands and knees, finally dragging himself to his feet to jog off through the rain and darkness toward Beaverton.

A hundred thoughts tangled themselves together in Ki's mind as he ran on toward the dim, distant lights of Beaverton. The throbbing of his brain didn't make it easy to untangle and organize them.

Jessica. His first thought was of her but he didn't even know where she was. She should be on the road to Denver, impossibly distant. Yoshiko was next in his thoughts, but again, he had no idea where she was—or only a distant idea.

Things had to be approached logically, then. He had to do what could be done with what he knew. That meant that Marshal King was first.

The rain had slowed to a dismal drizzle when Ki slogged into Beaverton, his legs trembling, his feet caked with gooey mud. The town seemed to be quiet, but armed men walked the plankwalks. Ki avoided them all as he worked his way to the marshal's office and walked to the front door.

He was poised to kill—every nerve of his body, each fiber of muscle, ready to take King apart piece by piece. He knocked on the door and stepped just enough to one side to be partly hidden by the shadows of the porch awning.

The door opened a bare inch.

"Who is—?" the man inside started to demand. But he never got a chance to finish the question. The door was kicked open and a powerful hand was wrapped around his throat. He fell back, pawing at his revolver, but that was useless. Ki's hand cracked down hard on his wrist and the gun clattered to the floor.

It wasn't King but another deputy Ki saw as he kicked the door shut behind him and marched the man backward across the office floor, his hand still locked around the deputy's throat.

"Where is the marshal?" Ki demanded as he backed the

deputy against the office desk, bending him over backward. Small, frightened eyes looked up at Ki from a suddenly perspiring face.

"I don't . . ." The deputy couldn't speak for a moment. Ki released his grip fractionally and waited. "I don't know. Out on patrol, I guess."

"I want to know now!" Ki said this very softly, but with a violent emphasis the man couldn't mistake. The hand that had been on his throat now slid to the knot of nerves at the base of the man's neck and squeezed very hard. Paralyzing pain shot through the deputy's body.

"Damn it all! I don't know where he is!" he shrieked. "He wasn't even here when I came on duty."

The hand squeezed just a little harder and the deputy slumped to the floor as his body succumbed to the pain.

"Kill him?" the man in the cell asked.

Ki glanced toward Dancer and shook his head. "Fainted. It happens. Where are the keys?"

"Bottom drawer. Ki . . . is it Jessica?" Dancer asked, reading the expression in Ki's eyes. "Is she all right?"

"I don't even know," Ki answered very slowly as he found the right key and swung the cell door open.

"Did you find Yoshiko?" Dancer snatched up his hat and then searched the office for his handgun. Ki just shook his head imperceptibly in answer to the question. Dancer borrowed a rifle from the marshal's gun rack and followed Ki to the door. The *te* master peered out at the darkened street and then whispered:

"Someone is coming up the plankwalk. It's not King. I think if we blow out the lamp and then just walk out we can get away with it."

"All right." Dancer snuffed out the hanging lantern by the door and then cocked his rifle, holding it beside his leg. "Just in case," he said with a grin, "we don't get away with it."

The two men slipped out in the darkness. Ki made a show of checking the door behind them and then they sauntered off, unchallenged.

Around two corners, Dancer touched Ki's arm. "Okay, where are we going?"

"To find Yoshiko. She's nearer than Jessica."

"You know where she is?"

"Not with any certainty, but something the deputies said to me gives me a fair idea. They told me Yoshiko would be fed and clothed and probably bedded."

"So?" Dancer was puzzled. His eyes lifted to the end of the alley, but it was only a dog trotting by he had heard.

"Do you think King would allow any thug at all to bed her? Or that the deputies would be so sure she would be fed and clothed, unless she was at King's own house?"

"I don't know, Ki. The marshal is the one behind all of this?"

"Yes."

"That shows me what kind of investigator I am," Dancer said unhappily.

"As good as Jessica and myself. It doesn't matter, let's find someone who knows where his house it."

"*That* I know," Dancer said. "Even incompetent investigators stumble across things now and then. A house outside of town a mile or so. Two storied, dark grey. Sits in a little canyon."

"You've seen it?"

"I can find it," Dancer said confidently. "I only hope the marshal's there himself."

They found two horses, conveniently hitched behind the Red Rooster Saloon, and borrowed them, riding off to the north through the downward sweep of the continuing rain. It took some time, but half an hour later they had found the house and were sitting on the cactus-studded hill above it, watching the dim lights burning in the windows.

"There'll be guards."

Ki just nodded. He preferred being silent until he had spotted the guards. Sound can carry for amazing distances, and even in the rain he was wary of speaking.

There was one man sheltered beneath the eaves of the house at the back. From time to time he shifted position. He was cold and bored and should be easy to take. There was a barn behind the house as well, but there was no sign of activity there. In the house itself everything seemed quiet as well, but if Yoshiko was a prisoner there, they could count on guards being about.

They waited and watched a while longer, hoping for some indication that King himself was there. But if he was, they couldn't tell. Finally, Ki nodded to Dancer and slipped from the back of the borrowed horse, leaving it ground-hitched. Then, with Ki leading the way, they slipped off down the hill through the rain-damp sage and sumac.

Reaching the flats, they moved even more cautiously, following a narrow gully to the cottonwoods that stood in a cluster thirty feet from the house. From there on it would be tricky.

Ki jabbed a finger toward the barn and its open loft. He meant to take the guard at the rear of the house silently, but if there were men watching from the barn it wouldn't play. Dancer nodded and settled himself prone beneath the trees, his sights on the barn.

Then Ki was off across the damp grass toward the house. He reached one corner of the building without being seen—at least no guns opened up.

Inside the house he heard small sounds. Music from a piano sounded briefly and then was cut off. Someone muttered and seemed to stamp away.

Ki eased toward the corner of the house and eased his head out. The guard was in the same position, leaning against the wall, his hat tugged down over his eyes, trying to stay out of the heaviest of the rain.

Ki was to him in three steps, and as his head came up, Ki's sidekick caught him in the diaphragm and he went down silently, gasping for breath.

Ki tugged him around the corner, bound and gagged him with his own belt and scarf, and lifted an arm toward the trees. In a minute Dancer, zigzagging as he ran, crossed the grass and joined Ki against the wall of the house.

Dancer's hat was gone now. Rain streamed across his

face, drifting his hair into his eyes. He held his rifle with both hands, his thumb locked around the hammer.

Ki whispered to him, "I'll take the front of the house. Stand by the back door and come in if you hear anything more than you hear now."

Dancer just nodded. He snatched up the guard's hat and slipped around the corner to take up his position. Ki started for the front of the house and nearly walked into a second guard.

The man started to call out, but Ki jammed his knee into his groin and the cry was throttled by pain. A *yonhon-nu-kite* blow finished the job.

Ki was nearly past the trellis before his eyes lifted upward, seeing its possibilities. It was nothing much, made of one-by-ones, but after testing it, he thought it would hold his weight. The rose which had grown there once was long dead.

Above Ki the eaves of the second story cut a straight line against the dark sky. He reached up, gripped a one-by, and started toward the roof.

Swinging onto the roof Ki paused, belly down, watching the lighted window five feet from his head. The rain began to increase again, driving down like buckshot, but he couldn't be sure it was loud enough to cover his movements.

He lifted his head slowly and, inching along toward the window, peered in over the sill. Beyond some tattered white lace curtains he could see a bed and dresser. The room looked like it had been furnished by a woman but used by a man. There were muddy boots on the braided rag carpet on the floor.

The door opened and Ki ducked his head. Above the hammering of the rain he could hear a voice briefly: ". . . do it his own damn self." Then the light went out and the door slammed shut.

Inside or out? Had the man come in and closed the door or gone out and closed it?

Inside or out?

It was a question which carried a lot of weight—Ki's

life or death. The man hadn't been King, of that Ki was sure. Exactly what he had been grumbling about was unimportant; all that mattered was the single question—inside or out?

Ki had heard no bedsprings sagging, heard no footsteps on the floor. Heard no opening and closing of drawers. The conclusion had to be, then, that the man had come in, blown out the lamp, and left.

Ki rose up and stepped toward the window. The shotgun blast tore away the window from its frame.

Chapter 14

The shotgun sheeted flame into the night. If it hadn't been for the sound of the hammers being drawn back, Ki would have been left headless. As it was, that telltale, chilling sound had sent him diving to the roof.

Both triggers. That thought flashed through Ki's mind instantly. That meant he had to reload; and whoever he was, he wasn't going to be fast enough.

Ki was up and through the window, a leaping *tobi-geri* kick sending the gunman flying back against the far wall, where his head thudded against plaster and he sagged to the floor.

Simultaneously Ki heard a shot downstairs and he knew Dancer, following instructions, had burst into the house. There was no time for caution. Ki flung the door open and stepped out, finding himself in a long, red-carpeted hallway.

Three strides on, a door opened out onto the hallway as Ki approached it. Ki's kick slammed the door back into the face of the man who had opened it, and the man fell to the floor, his face a bloody mask. He wasn't quite out and Ki picked his head up by the greasy hair and asked:

"Where is she—the Japanese girl?"

The outlaw was in no shape to be evasive. "Cellar," he said, looking fearfully into Ki's slashing eyes.

"And King?"

"Don't know."

Ki believed him, because the answer to the first question had come so easily. He threw the man's head back against the floor, rose, and pivoted, moving toward the

135

door like a stalking cat. Below, three rapid shots were fired. That meant that Dancer was still alive.

At the head of a curving staircase Ki paused and crouched. Below, a gunman behind an upturned sofa was firing his handgun at an unseen target. The *shuriken* sang through the air and struck the outlaw's spine, severing the cord, and the man flung himself backward in an involuntary spasm.

When he had stopped his writhing Ki took a chance and called out, "Dancer?"

"Here, Ki."

"Any more of them down there?"

"I don't think so. Come on ahead; I'll cover you."

Ki eased down the stairs to the well-furnished but neglected parlor below. Dancer, his face still rain-damp and smudged, met him, rifle in hand.

"Find her?" Dancer inquired.

"No. She's supposed to be in the cellar, wherever that is."

A little searching around brought them to the door off the kitchen pantry which led down to the cellar. Dancer started to follow Ki, but the *te* master stopped him.

"If there are others outside they'll be coming now."

Dancer nodded and found a protected place to stand watch. Ki dropped down into the cellar, which was unlighted. He saw a candle on the wall and struck a match. The flaring light showed a small door to the right and Ki kicked it in.

"My warrior, I knew you would find me soon!"

Yoshiko had her hair combed and pinned, and she was wearing a white woman's blue gingham dress. Ki frowned. "You are all right?"

"Of course, my samurai."

She came to Ki and put her arms around his waist. Ki's mouth tightened a little more. The woman was playing a child's game in a grown-up world. Her experiences had taught her nothing. Maybe the master was right; maybe Yoshiko did belong cloistered in the monastery, away from real life.

"Come on, we must go now," Ki said, turning her by the arm.

"Where are you taking me?"

136

"I don't know." He practically dragged her from the room and up the stairs. Dancer glanced at Ki and grinned.

"No sign of anyone yet, Ki."

Ki glanced at the kitchen door. "Is there another way?" he asked Yoshiko.

"I don't know. I have seen nothing, Ki. They made me wear a blindfold when they brought me here."

"Not much time to look around, Ki," Dancer said. "Risk it?"

Ki nodded. He didn't like the idea much. If there were others outside they would be watching the entrances. "We'll try it. Blow out the lamp and get in the window, Michael."

Dancer did as he was told while Yoshiko watched, curiously. Ki gripped the girl's wrist tightly and led her to the door. When Dancer was in position he put his hand on the brass knob and swung the door open, holding Yoshiko to one side.

It was like lighting a fuse. The night exploded with gunfire as bullets sang through the kitchen, ringing off hanging kettles and ripping at the lintel.

Dancer opened up from the window, aiming his fire at the muzzle flashes, working the lever of his Winchester as rapidly as possible. Ki rolled out the door, taking Yoshiko with him. The girl cried out in fear, but had no choice but to go along, rolling into the cold mud outside, scrambling to her feet to run with Ki into the shadows of the trees.

There they paused, catching their breath as Ki looked back at the house. Now to get Dancer out of there.

He didn't have a gun, but he had other tools to work with. He took Yoshiko firmly by both shoulders and whispered savagely, "This time do as I say. Stay here until I return."

She nodded her head meekly and watched as her samurai wove his way through the trees toward the snipers' position.

They weren't hard to find, even in the near-total darkness. One of them had been tagged by Dancer's bullets, and he was moaning his pain to the night while the others tried to quiet him.

The two remaining men never had a chance. Behind a fallen log, rifles and attention fixed on the door to the house, they never saw the shadowy figure emerge for the rain and darkness to become in death-dealing spirit.

The man on the ground with Dancer's bullet in him looked up with pleading eyes at Ki, pleading for mercy, for his life; but it was useless. Dancer's bullet had taken him through the lungs and he was going to go anyway, more painfully. Ki finished him with a merciful death-stroke.

"Dancer!" Ki called just once and the investigator emerged from the house, trusting Ki.

Yoshiko waited as if rooted to the spot where Ki had left her, her hands wringing. Maybe, Ki thought, we are making progress.

Dancer, hobbling a little, panting loudly, found them in another minute. "What now?" he asked. "Wait for King to show?"

"If you want," Ki replied. "I am going to look for Jessica."

"She's probably in Denver," Dancer said.

"She may be in Denver." Ki looked southward. "Nevertheless I am going to look for her. Will you get our horses?"

"There's some closer," Dancer said. "Three of them. Or are you going to get rid of the girl?"

Ki looked at Yoshiko, who had her head down, her hands still clasped. And where could he put her? Who could he trust to watch over her? He didn't like the decision he had reached.

"She goes with us."

Jessica hung on to the wagon for as long as she could. The storm wrapped around them like a dark, rustling curtain. The silver wagon jolted over the rutted, muddy road. It was obvious where they were heading—Castle Wells, counting on the rain to erase the deep tracks the wagon was making.

Her hands were cramped and torn, her ankles bruised. Rounding a sharp upward bend, the outriders threw ropes onto the wagon to help tow it up the grade. It was then, while all of the outlaws were in front of the wagon, that Jessica released her grip and fell heavily into the mud beneath the wagon.

She rolled to one side of the road quickly, stopping in a brush-clotted gully only a few feet from the wagon.

"What was that?" she heard one of the outlaws ask.

"What?" someone else responded with irritation.

"Thought I saw something beside the road."

"Getting jittery, Bob?" The other one laughed. "Who do you expect out here, the cavalry, maybe?"

"What's the matter?" a third voice boomed.

"Nothin'. Bob's seeing spooks."

"Get your asses up here and help out instead of screwin' around."

The men muttered something and rode off toward the head of the column, and Jessica let out a deep breath of relief.

It seemed hours that she lay there in the cold mud, the rain falling on her back, before they got the wagon up around the bend and were gone, leaving only the sound of the storm behind.

Slowly Jessica got to her feet, rubbing her hands together and then trying to work circulation back into her thighs, which felt frozen to the bone. She stood in the rain then, looking ahead and back down the trail.

"Great," she muttered. She had made her escape, but what was she going to do now? Start back through the rain toward Beaverton, across open land? She'd be lucky if she made it a mile or two before she just fell down exhausted.

The distant tiny glow seemed to answer her question. She wasn't sure she saw it at first as the clouds shifted and parted, but then she was. Somewhere up ahead a lamp was burning, or a small fire. There wasn't much choice—she started that way on wooden legs.

And just where was Ki tonight? And Dancer? She couldn't count on either of them to help her; that much was certain. Michael Dancer was almost certainly in jail; Ki still somewhere near Beaverton. They weren't going to find her, even if they looked, and she had no sure idea that they were going to be looking on this night.

The light was nearer and Jessica could now see that it was a ranch house. She paused, holding her side as she tried to breathe normally.

"Damned if it isn't," she said to herself at last. She had recognized the house finally. She and Ki had stopped there on their way to Castle Wells. The cantankerous old man with the ready rifle lived there alone.

She hesitated, thinking it over. Looking around, Jessica saw nothing but the dark form of the low hills which sheltered Castle Wells. Her teeth were chattering, her body shivering with the cold.

There wasn't a lot of choice. Jessie started on down the mud-washed slope toward the ranch house.

Walking to the sheltered front door, she rapped three times and waited. Nothing. Nervously she looked around, shivering more violently as a gust of cold wind raked her body.

Another three raps brought a muffled grunt from inside and the approach of footsteps over creaking floorboards. The door opened a crack and the rancher peered out, his gray-browed eyes narrowing, his mouth tightening so that deep grooves formed around it. In his hand was an old Colt Navy revolver.

"What is it?" he snapped. She couldn't tell if he recognized her or not in that light. Probably not, she decided.

"I'd like to come in. I'm freezing and wet clean through," Jessica answered. Still the man hesitated suspiciously.

"All right," he said finally with disgust. The door swung wide open briefly and Jessie squeezed through into the interior of the musty sweat- and tobacco-smelling house. Muddy boots stood on the plank floor; a whisky bottle, half-empty, sat beside an overstuffed red chair, which had both arms split. A fire burned low in a stone fireplace.

The door banged shut and Jessica turned to look the man in the face. He was irritated at having his solitary life interrupted, wary, and maybe a little embarrassed at the state of the house.

There was also a look in his eyes which Jessica had seen thousands of times in a thousand places. He was well aware that the young woman before him was beautiful, and some deep, nearly latent, sexuality was creeping nearer the surface. The look deepened when Jessie took off her soaked jacket and hung it near the fire. Her blouse, soaked through, showed clearly the outline of her full young breasts and taut nipples.

He watched Jessica closely as she stood with her back to the fire, trying to warm herself. He placed the revolver on a table where a filthy tin plate rested next to an empty can of beans, its lid crudely sawed open with a knife blade.

"Where in hell'd you come from?" the old man asked, crossing to his chair to sag into it and pick up his whisky bottle. He drank directly from it and coughed.

"My horse threw me," Jessie tried. "Lightning struck close by us. He took off and I was stranded."

The man nodded, not believing it. Finally it came back to him, and a finger, its tip missing, lifted toward her. "I seen you before. Came by with some Indian fellow, looking for Castle Wells."

"That's right," Jessica answered, turning her front toward the fire now.

"How'd you make out over there?" he asked, taking another swallow. The stuff was so raw that the smell carried to Jessica's nostrils and burned them.

"We took your advice. Talked it over and decided it wasn't safe, so we didn't go."

"That right?" the man said with mild interest and disbelief.

"Yes." Jessica turned again and offered one of her quick, friendly smiles. "Have you got a towel around here?" She tugged at her hair and the old man, after a moment's thought, put his bottle down and dragged himself from his chair. He returned in a minute with a towel that was only slightly grimy, and Jessica started toweling her head vigorously.

"Trying to get back to Beaverton, are you?" the man asked. His eyes had gotten bleary and more than a little red.

"That's right."

He nodded and glanced at the door. "Where's that friend of yours, the Indian?"

"He'll be along," Jessie said, not liking the tone of the question or the growing interest in the rancher's eyes as he studied her body. "I'd like to hire a horse from you—I've got the money."

141

"None to hire."

"I can buy one, then. I'll give you a good price."

"We'll talk about it when your friend shows up—he's lost too, is he?" the man asked.

"No, he'll be along. I want to be ready to travel." She held her hands before the fire, feeling the eyes on her back and ass.

"You can't ride out again tonight. Weather's going to get worse. Stay here till morning."

"I really can't." Jessica turned and tried a smile again. She got none in response; only that same hungry stare.

"Don't make sense to ride on," the rancher said. Then he got back to his drinking and staring.

Jessica had walked into a bad situation and knew it. The fire caused steam to rise from her jeans and blouse as she stood there measuring the man. Harmless—maybe. You couldn't blame someone for looking. But there was something deeper and unhealthy in those red-rimmed eyes.

"All right," she said lightly after a minute, "I guess you're right. I'll stay here if you've got a place for me to sleep."

"You can have the bed," he answered, inclining his head toward a back room. "I'll sleep out here."

"Fine." Jessie walked around the front room, hands behind her back, curious look in place as she examined the antlers on the wall, the old army saber. "Have you got anything to eat?" she asked.

"Right out there—maybe a woman can rustle up something from what I've got. Me, I just had beans."

He got to his feet very deliberately, eyes gleaming, as Jessica walked toward the table and the small pantry. He was three steps away from her before she turned and the eyes lost all of their glow. That big Navy Colt revolver was in the lady's hands, the hammer drawn back. And she looked like she knew how to use it.

"Look, little lady . . ."

"Listen, mister. All I want's a horse and I'll go. I'll pay you."

142

"I thought you was staying here, you know—waiting for your friend," the rancher protested, his eyes still fixed on the muzzle of the big Colt in her small hands.

"Afraid not. I don't know what your thoughts are; maybe I'm reading you wrong, maybe not—but I'm not about to spend the night here. I've got things to do."

The man squinted at her closely. Weren't her hands shaking a little now? Maybe she didn't have what it took after all. Maybe . . . He took one more step and the gun exploded with thunder and flame, the sound deafening in the enclosed room. The bullet whined off the stone of the fireplace and scattered embers across the room.

He stopped, his hand still half-raised. "All right, have it your way, bitch. That's what I get for trying to help a woman out," he growled.

"What do you want for a horse?" Jessie asked, reaching into her jeans, keeping the Colt steady with one hand.

"I got two. Roan's steady, gray's faster. Both of 'em five years old."

"A hundred dollars?" Jessica suggested, and the gleam was back in the old man's eyes. A different sort of gleam which deepened as he saw the gold in Jessie's hand. He had given thirty for the gray, twenty-five for the roan. Hell, he was going to get something for this efforts after all. Not what he had anticipated, but something.

"Sold. Now get out of here, will you? Take your jacket, leave my Colt, and scoot. Horse is around back, in the shed. Take your choice and ride out. Leave me alone."

"I am. The Colt will be in the shed—unless you want to sell it too."

"Only handgun I got. I got an old Spencer rifle?" he said, making it a question. "Somewhere thirty rounds or so for it."

"Get it," Jessica said.

She watched him as he crossed to a cluttered cabinet and rummaged around in it, bringing up an old, but cleaned and oiled Spencer repeater and a tattered box of .56-caliber cartridges. He started to load the gun, but Jessica stopped him with a motion of the pistol.

"That'll do," she said.

"Sure." He shrugged and handed over the cartridges, which she tucked under her arm, and the rifle. Then, easing toward her jacket, Jessie put it on, dropping the big buffalo gun's shells into her pocket. The rancher watched each movement like a cat watching a bird.

Jessie eased by him, dropped the gold coins on the table, and then, with a nod, eased out the door. She waited on the porch for a minute, but he didn't try to follow her.

The rain still fell as Jessica walked to the rundown shed and saddled the gray horse. Leading it out into the rain she flipped the unloaded revolver back into the shed, swung aboard, and, with the big Spencer repeater in one hand, heeled the horse out of the yard.

A quarter of a mile on she slowed the horse and finally halted it.

Which way?

Beaverton was miles away, Castle Wells half as far. To ride toward the outlaw camp was crazy, but what was there to be gained by returning to Beaverton? She wouldn't be able to raise a posse, couldn't wire for help. Her father, Alex Starbuck, had always told her that a person does his own work, that he or she was ultimately responsible for events, not those you enlisted for help and paid for it. It was her silver, her mine, and maybe her fault that men had died on the plains that night. An anger was building in Jessica, and there was nothing she could do to fight it back. She looked back toward Beaverton once more and then made her decision.

She turned the gray toward the east and started up the trail toward Castle Wells through the driving night rain.

★

Chapter 15

Ki couldn't see any sign of life in or around the small, squat building beyond the trees. A few miles ago they had passed a burned-out, abandoned ranch, and Dancer made a guess:

"Just a line shack from that old ranch, Ki."

The *te* master nodded. "I think so too."

The storm was worse than ever, blustering and blowing, sending fountains of lightning showering across the skies. Yoshiko was ready to fall from her horse from sheer weariness. As little as Ki wanted to, he recognized that they were going to have to hole up if possible. The horses were worn out, the storm violent, and they were lost. They had to face that as well. None of them recognized the land around them; in the darkness they had wandered far from the trail.

"We're going to have to chance it, Ki!" Dancer said above the howl of the wind which rattled through the oaks. "We're not going to find the trail tonight."

"No. We have to chance it."

It was Dancer who went down to the shack, cautiously kicked open the door, which sagged on leather hinges, and inspected the shack as well as he could. A jagged bolt of lightning briefly illuminated the place with eerie blue-white light and Dancer saw the lantern, on its side on a table.

He picked up the lamp and shook it. A dollop of kerosene sloshed around inside it and his match brought the flat wick of the lamp to life. The place was dusty, but surprisingly untouched by nature and time. A cot, only its leather strapping left for a mattress, rested against one wall. The table had two chairs for rickety companions. It would have to do.

"Looks safe enough, dry as we can expect," he reported to Ki.

"We will stop?" Yoshiko asked.

"We will stop."

Behind the house was a lean-to, sagging badly due to one tilted upright pole. Ki and Dancer got it straightened a little and put the horses in out of the rain. Then they went into the line shack, Ki standing surveying it with hands on hips for a minute before saying, "I have slept in worse places."

"Are they looking for us?" Yoshiko asked, her almond eyes fixed on Ki's. "The marshal and Takahashi?"

"I don't think so. They would not know where to look —and on a night like this they would not find us anyway."

Yoshiko seemed to relax a little. Her body sagged with weariness and she looked toward the sagging, uncomfortable looking cot. "If we only had a blanket."

"We'll have to do the best we can," Ki answered. He spoke to Dancer then: "I can't believe anyone could find us, Michael. Still, I'm going to stand watch up in the trees."

"All right." Dancer shrugged and yawned at once. "Wake me in a few hours. I'll spell you."

They heard Yoshiko shriek with glee, and glancing that way, saw her hold up two blankets; motheaten and dusty, they still beat nothing on that bitterly cold, rainy night.

Ki waited until she had made up her bed, and Dancer had made his on the floor. Then he slipped out again into the night. It was an empty world then, filled with only nature's sounds. There might not have been another human being on the face of the earth. There was only the wind soughing through the trees, the constant sound of rain, the occasional explosion of thunder and lightning.

He squatted on his heels beneath an oak and let his eyes and ears do the work for him. His mind drifted from point to point. He was in the monastery once again, watching the young Yoshiko play, hearing the chants of the Master.

The Master.

Ki felt as if he were rebelling against his father, for the Master had been as much a father to him as the Yankee sea captain he hardly recalled.

Yes, a father. And even though Ki knew he had done no wrong, he felt the guilt a son feels when he has displeased the father he wanted so much to please.

Twice there had been violence between them, and there would be violence again. The Master no longer listened. He was a stalking killing thing and Ki was his target. It could only end in death for one of them.

For the first time Ki realized that fully, knowing that he was incapable of killing the Master, that the Master was equally incapable of forgetting a supposed slight, of forgiving.

Where was Jessica on this night? He could not forget her either, or dismiss the thought that he had not done his duty, the duty given to him by Alex Starbuck himself: to watch over his beautiful and too impetuous daughter.

Ki found himself growing tense with these thoughts, found his pulse lifting. That did him no good, did no good for anyone at all. In calmness was productive thought, useful action. He began to slowly chant the old prayers, those taught him once long ago in a far-away monastery.

"Ki?"

When Dancer found Ki he was motionless, soaked to the bone. His eyes were completely alert; while Dancer did not think he had been sleeping, he had no idea what Ki had actually been doing. Meditation was something Michael Dancer had never encountered before, and likely never would again.

"Yes, Dancer. Is it time?" The tall man uncoiled and stood before Dancer.

"You didn't come down and wake me up. I thought I'd better see what was happening. You can't stand watch all night, Ki."

"No." There was no point in explaining to Dancer that Ki was nearly as well rested after his meditations as he would have been after eight hours of deep sleep.

"Yoshiko's still sleeping soundly. Doesn't look like the storm's going to let up, does it?"

Ki glanced skyward. "Not for a while."

There was still that strange distant look about Ki. Dancer guessed it was weariness. He slapped Ki on the shoulder. "Get some sleep now, will you?"

"Yes, I will sleep now."

Ki walked away down the slope and Dancer watched him for a minute, still puzzled. Then he tugged down his sleeves for warmth and leaned against the damp, rough bark of the huge oak to wait out his watch.

Ki walked swung open the door to the line shack and closed it gently. The lamp burned as low as possible without going out in the far corner, the wick fizzling and sparking, a smoky column of illumination rising from it, painting the wall with shifting shadows.

Yoshiko was naked on the bed, her arms outspread.

"I have been awake a long while, waiting or you."

"Go to sleep," Ki said, shedding his vest and shirt.

"You are tired, samurai?" the girl asked, sitting up on the bed. Her breasts, conical, firm, tipped with long, dark nipples, stood out clearly.

"Yes," Ki answered, turning his back. "I am tired."

He walked to where Dancer's bed had been, and rolled up in the blanket. Yoshiko slipped from the bed to cross the cold cabin floor.

"You are not tired, but angry," she said, standing over him.

"Yes, angry," Ki said. Still, his eyes ran up her golden thighs to the thick patch of dark hair which formed a triangle at the base of her flat belly.

"But why?" she sank to her knees, her breasts inches from his eyes. Tilting his chin up she repeated the question, "Why?"

"Because," Ki said carefully, "the Master and I have become enemies where once we were friends. This, Yoshiko, is something you are responsible for."

"For loving too much, for following you to America?" she asked as if she truly didn't understand.

148

"For coming to America," Ki answered, He was aware of the heat of her body, of her hand's touch as it slipped from his chin to his shoulder and rested there. Sensations Ki did not want to respond to began to course through his body, centering in his groin, where the ancient swelling sensation began.

"I understand." Yoshiko sat on her heels and clasped her hands together at her crotch. "It was said to me: a woman is a man's only curse, and woman his only comfort. Now I shall give you comfort, Ki, and take away the curse I have placed on you."

Mentally, Ki argued, but he did nothing to fight the progression of her hands as they rested on his knees and slipped up across his hard-muscled thighs to his groin.

"You have already been damned, Ki. For one single night of lovemaking. What can another night add except pleasure?"

Her mouth bent to Ki's and her lips parted slowly like an opening flower, dewy and warm, and Ki was too much of a man to resist their touch and the urging of her fingers against his growing erection.

Yoshiko smiled softly and rose. She was naked before him, proud of her new-found womanliness, of her warrior. She turned slowly and then bent over, resting her palms against the floor. Ki stood, shedding his trousers, and moved to her.

He moved against Yoshiko's ass, warm flesh against warm flesh, his hands resting on her. Still she held her position, hands on the floor, but her legs shifted slightly so that her sex was open to Ki, who explored her gently with his fingers before pressing against her again, his shaft finding the soft entrance to her body.

He was gentle and very slow, touching her with the head of his maleness before entering her an inch at a time, drawing a shudder from her with each small thrust.

He felt her body loosen and become incredibly moist. Still Yoshiko had her palms against the floor, her hair fanned out against it. Now one arm reached back and she

149

cradled Ki's sack in her palm as his last small thrust put him in up to the base of his swollen member.

Ki held himself still for a long minute, his hands running over her sleek ass and thighs as Yoshiko touched him where he entered her, caressed her own body with knowing fingers. Her thighs began to tremble and as Ki moved inside of her she gasped, her hand falling back to the floor, bracing herself for Ki's onslaught.

He bucked against her steadily, hearing her gasps and moans as he gripped her hips and lifted her body against his, feeling the surge of need building deep in his loins.

Yoshiko cried out once, loudly, and beat one hand against the floor, clutching at his leg as Ki finished with a series of furious thrusts, finding an explosive climax.

He held her to him, both of them trembling, until Yoshiko, panting, nodded her head and rose, turning to cling to Ki in the night, her body overheated, her arms shining deeply. She kissed him with parted lips which breathed steam into the air, and Ki swept her up into his arms, carrying her to her bed where he placed her down like a child.

"We must never part, Ki," she said, running a finger over his lips. "You will never go, will you?"

Ki didn't answered. He turned away and dressed before lying down with Dancer's blanket. She watched him until the fuel in the lantern finally burned out and darkness closed off her vision.

Dancer let Ki sleep until the hour before dawn. Then he crept into the line shack and, with a glance at the sleeping Yoshiko, crossed to Ki and touched his shoulder. Ki's eyes opened instantly.

"Trouble?"

"No. It'll be dawn soon. I thought we should be ready to travel at first light."

"Yes." Ki yawned. "You are right."

"We'll have some trouble with the weather, Ki," Dancer said as the Japanese rolled out of the blankets and got to his feet.

"Is it still raining?"

"No." Dancer nodded toward the window, where snow

could be seen falling gently, steadily. It was the last thing they needed. "Ki, the woman—how about leaving her here? It's out of the way. If she'd stay put, she'd be all right."

"It won't work, Dancer."

"Why not? After we find Jessica we can come back this way and pick her up."

Ki lifted an eyebrow. "And if we don't come back at all?"

"Then she's better off here too, isn't she?"

Ki shook his head. He wanted nothing more than to find a safe place to leave Yoshiko, but this wasn't it. She was just going to have to tag along and take her chances with them.

The sky was gray at dawn, with drifting snow falling in wind-formed swirls. The trees were bleak and gray. The horses were in no mood to travel.

They rode out of the line shack as a brief, dull flash of orange showed through the clouds and then hid itself away again. The snow kept falling. It was going to be a long, cold day.

"We won't find those wagon tracks now," Dancer was saying. He had his collar turned up, his hat pulled low. As he spoke, steam formed on his lips. "I doubt we'll ever catch up with—"

And then they both saw it. Sitting splay-wheeled in the snow, one of the silver wagons appeared below them. Scattered around the wagon were dark forms like fallen tree branches. But they weren't branches.

They had all halted their horses on the low knoll. Now Dancer shouted out "Jessica," his voice anguished and breaking, and he started down the slope at a dead run, his horse's hooves kicking up fans of snow.

Ki was right behind him as he reached the wagon and swung down, searching the bodies which lay scattered in the snow. She wasn't there—that much was good news. The rest of it was tragedy.

Yoshiko, her hair frosted with snow, stood staring around in bewilderment at the death surrounding her.

Twisted and frozen men were scattered across the earth around the broken wagon. Farther upslope there was another group of bodies, some of them Japanese tiger-clan men.

The snow had covered much but they could still see furrows where the second wagon had been driven off.

"Maybe they fought them off," Dancer suggested. "Beat the outlaws back and continued toward Denver."

"No," Ki said. "Count the dead. They're all dead except for Jessica."

"Prisoner? You think they have her prisoner, Ki?"

"There's no telling. She may have gotten away and started back toward Beaverton. We'll never find her tracks now."

"What do we do then?"

"Go after the outlaws and the silver," Ki said. "Maybe we will find Jessica with them."

"You know where to find them?"

"Yes," Ki said quietly, lifting his eyes southward. "I know where to find them, Michael Dancer."

They returned to their horses then, mounted, and began riding toward the jumbled hills and Castle Wells beyond. There, if anywhere, they would find Jessica. The day grew colder yet. The snow fell heavily, obscuring the landscape, but Ki knew the way now; he knew the road to hell.

By the time they reached the southern trail the snow had stopped. Now and then bright sunlight broke through the clouds and made a mirror of the snowy fields.

"I don't like taking the woman any farther, Ki," Dancer said.

Nor did Ki, but he didn't know what to do with the woman. Yoshiko had been silent since she had viewed the battlefield. Maybe now she knew, knew that no man was above death, not even her samurai lover. Maybe now she had become a little less of a girl and a little more of a woman.

Ki first spotted the town by the rising fingers of wood smoke. The outlaws were gathered around their iron stoves, warm and dry, drinking whisky, laughing, congratulating themselves on another successful robbery.

While good men lay dead in the snow.

The outlaws sat smug and secure behind the hills in their fortress, confident that the law was not going to do anything, and that no one else could. They ruled this corner of the state. King and Takahashi were like Japan's ancient robber barons—a law to themselves.

The longer Ki sat his horse and looked at the town the madder he got. "The bastards," he said at last, "will pay. Every one of them."

"And we're going to do it ourselves?" Dancer asked bitterly.

Ki slowly turned his head. His eyes were unusally bright. "That's right; we'll do it ourselves. There isn't anyone else, is there, Dancer?"

The snow had begun again, and hard, throwing a white screen across the valley before Ki and Dancer started down toward the outlaw town. Yoshiko still tagged along, and Ki hated the necessity of that. Again, outside of plopping her down in the snow and telling her to stay put—which probably wouldn't work anyway—there was nothing to do with her but let her follow.

The big house was to their right and not far below them. Ki's idea was to take out Takahashi first, cut the head off the outlaw beast that was prowling the territory. There would also be important records in the house, if Takahashi was the businessman most Japanese are. Records of where the silver had gone, who had purchased it from the outlaws, and how it had been transported to wherever it went from here. Ki wanted those records. He wanted to smash the entire organization behind the robberies.

He had to find Jessica.

If she was there she was likely a prisoner and one not apt to be treated well at all.

Yoshiko stepped into a snow-covered hole and fell with a small cry. Ki cursed silently and helped her up. Before them, within a stone's throw, was one of the rock outbuildings of the house. Ki motioned for Yoshiko to stay well behind as he slowed his own pace and looked ahead, trying to peer through the veil of heavy snow, to spot any watching guards.

They reached the south wall of the stone house without incident. Ki couldn't even make out the big house from there. The day was winter-silent. No one seemed to be moving around the grounds or inside the house.

He nodded to Dancer, pointed toward the corner of the stone house, and moved toward it, wanting a better look. He walked right in to the muzzle of the gun.

Chapter 16

Jessica felt her heart leap into her throat. The big Spencer repeater's trigger was cool under her finger. She leaped back and started to squeeze off a shot before she cursed softly and said: "Ki!" She lowered the rifle. "I came that close to shooting you. You're not supposed to be anywhere near here."

"Nor are you," Ki said gently. He hugged her briefly and drew her back around the corner of the house. Dancer was to her in two strides, holding her tight while the snow fell.

"What happened?" he asked, and she explained.

"Very foolish, Jessie," Ki said, shaking his head.

"Yeah?" She smiled. "What about you coming out here looking for me? I was just so damned mad I wanted to do something. I wasn't going to go crawling back to Beaverton with my tail between my legs. What exactly is your plan anyway, Ki?"

He sketched it out and she whistled. "Your mind must work like mine. The first part's out, though. No point in going into Takahashi's house."

"Why?"

"I've been there. It's empty. Furniture's gone, desk cleaned out—don't look at me that way. I know it was dumb to go in alone, but I watched the place for a long time first, and when I didn't see any guards, or anyone else, I decided to try it."

"Where could he have gone?" Dancer asked. "And why?"

"Why isn't too hard to figure," Ki opined. "There just won't be any more silver shipments for Centennial, Mi-

155

chael. Things are closed down there for the foreseeable future. No sense maintaining this expensive setup. Besides, they must feel it's time go on to the second step."

"The second step? What do you mean, Ki?" Dancer asked.

"They want the Centennial. The whole works. Takahashi and King are going to try buying it."

"Probably through a bank, or the agent they've been funneling the stolen silver off to," Jessica continued the thought. "But it won't work. I sure as hell won't sell it."

"Maybe they think you're dead," Dancer commented.

"Or intend to make sure you are," Ki added. "I still want to look around the house, Jessie." He glanced at Yoshiko. "If you two will wait here with her."

"All right, if you think there's anything to be gained by it. Just what is Yoshiko doing here? Where was she? And Dancer—how did you get sprung?"

Those were questions that could be left for Michael Dancer to answer. Ki slipped out from behind the corner of the stone house into the driving snow, and worked his way toward the main house. He moved with as much caution as ever. Because Jessica had seen no one didn't necessarily mean there was no one there. He could see virtually nothing through the snow. Someone could easily have returned.

But inside the house it was cold and dark and still. Ki walked up the stairs to Takahashi's office and entered it. The desk drawers were open, the wall safe empty and open wide. In the corner was a filing cabinet. It too was cleaned out. Ki paused before the cabinet and then ran a hand over its varnished wooden side. The lettering on the face of the cabinet was still clearly visible.

When the curtain behind him moved he thought of the wind. He didn't expect the body to topple forward and flop onto the floor. There was a ledge behind the curtains and that was where the body had been lodged. Ki toed the corpse and it rolled over, face up.

Takahashi had been paid.

Someone had stuck the Japanese in the side of the neck with a narrow-bladed knife. It had been effective enough.

The rest of the house seemed to be empty as well. As Jessica had told them, even the furniture had been taken away. With a cursory look at the empty cells below ground, Ki went out again, crossed the snowy yard, and rejoined Dancer and Jessie behind the rock house. Yoshiko, squatting in the snow, looked up with anxious eyes. For the time being Ki ignored her.

"Nothing there," Ki reported. "They left Takahashi behind."

"Dead?"

"That's right. They don't need to organize the tiger clan anymore. They just don't need him."

"King, you mean."

"King, yes. It has to be. King—and his flunkies, who are likely to find themselves in the same position as Takahashi if they aren't careful. The marshal doesn't mind killing in the least."

"I wish to hell we knew where he was," Dancer said. "Beaverton?"

"No, not now. I think I know, though. Do you know where Grand Forks is?"

"Grand Forks?" Jessica asked. "We rode through there, didn't we, Ki?"

"But why there?" Dancer asked.

"There's a cabinet in Takahashi's office. You can just make out the lettering: 'Bank of Grand Forks.' I think we'll find King in Grand Forks, and find out where the silver's been going as well."

"Its a long ride," Dancer said, "But we can try it."

Jessica put a hand on Dancer's arm. "Not just yet, Michael. Right, Ki? We're not quite finished here."

"No." Ki looked toward the town, invisible behind the wash of white the storm drifted past them. "We're not quite finished here."

"You two aren't serious, are you?" Dancer looked from one face to the other. Both Jessica and Ki wore the same set expression. "For God's sake, Jessie! Ki—you were talking about destroying the town, but you can't have meant it. The three of us against an army of outlaws?"

157

"I meant it," Ki said gravely. "I don't know how we're going to do it, but we're going to destroy this nest of snakes. They've hurt too many people for too long."

"I've got something that might help," Jessica said with a wink. Ki and Dancer just shrugged and followed as she inclined her head and walked to the door of the stone house. "Didn't you ever wonder what was in this place, why it was so far away from the main house? I did." Jessica swung the door open and went in. Ki noticed that she had jimmied the lock earlier. "I had some time to look around," she told them. "Hold it, Michael!"

Dancer had struck a match. It went out quickly enough as he spotted the cases marked "Dynamite" on the floor.

"Plenty of it," Jessica said. "I don't know what they intended to use it for, but I know where I'd like to stick it."

Ki was prying open a crate, placing the fuse aside. Dancer was still doubtful. "This is something, Ki, but we can't just go down there and start blowing everything up. We wouldn't have a chance."

Ki rose, his face as grim as Dancer had ever seen it. "You are very probably right, Michael, but we're going to try." He glanced at Jessica and she nodded her answer. "We are going to have our try at it."

"You're both crazy," Dancer said, his voice soft and astonished. Then the old grin came back. "But if you're going to try it, I guess I'm in on it."

"Jessica, this will be very dangerous. If—"

"No, you don't, Ki. I was here first. I'm in on it."

"Yoshiko?" Dancer asked.

Yes, Yoshiko. It was time to put her somewhere and hope for the best. This last step was too much beyond her capabilities. Ki crouched beside her and took her small hands.

"I want you to take the horses and go to the north end of town. You remember the trail we followed out of Castle Wells last time, the little ledge?" Yes, she remembered that. Her eyes glowed with the recollection. "Go there then, Yoshiko. Go there and do nothing to give yourself

158

away. We will join you in three or four hours. You'll know when we're coming."

"Ki . . . ?"

"You will do as I ask you this time, won't you?"

She didn't answer with words. She nodded, pulled herself upright, kissed Ki on the lips, and was gone, scrambling upslope through the snow. Ki shrugged. "That was all there was to do."

With Yoshiko gone they got down to the business at hand. Dancer didn't have much faith at all in the idea. "It will all have to go up at once, won't it? I mean, they'll be alerted if it doesn't."

"If they are alerted, what can they do but run?" Ki asked. He was uncoiling lengths of fuse as Jessica bundled the sticks of dynamite together with friction tape.

"If the snow keeps up we won't have any trouble reaching town, at least," Dancer said from the doorway of the stone house. "Probably not even much trouble moving around in the town itself. But getting out, Ki . . ."

"Yes," Ki agreed. "Getting out is the problem." Because if things went right the outlaw town would find itself destroyed, men killed, and the gunmen would swarm out of Castle Wells in all directions looking for their attackers.

Ki took the time to sketch out the plan of the town as well as he could remember it, with Jessica and Dancer making a few corrections. Then the targets were marked.

"The hotel, the saloons; those are the most important targets. After that it's as you like it; destroy everything that's standing."

Jessica said, "Ki, I'd like to get the horses out of town first. At least those in the stable. First, I don't like seeing them hurt, second, it'll keep the pursuit slowed down."

"You have an idea?" Ki asked.

"Open the gate and let them out," Jessie said with a smile.

"It'll have to be done after the charges are set. You'll increase your own risk, you know."

"And mine," Dancer said. "I'll be with her."

Ki nodded, rose, and picked up the burlap sack full of

159

dynamite he had packed and ready. Jessie and Ki each had a sack of their own. Dancer fixed his to his belt to leave his hands free. Then, one by one, they slipped out of the house and started down toward the outlaw town.

Ki started at the north end of town, Jessie and Dancer at the south. The nerves were jumping even in Ki's normally imperturbable body. There was always the chance of getting caught. Even being detained meant the risk of blowing up yourself—or your friends—in a flaming flash.

The snow was six inches deep underfoot. Ki's tracks were plainly visible in the snow as he crouched in the alley behind a saloon called the Medallion, unwinding fuse which he set in a bundle of six sticks of dynamite. This fuse, being the first, would be the longest. Ki gave himself five minutes of fuse, tucked the dynamite behind a water barrel, and lit a match.

The fuse hissed away, a deadly sparkling snake. Ki started on at a trot now, his heart pounding. This wasn't his favorite game. Explosives are unpredicatable. If that fuse was too fast or . . . The outlaw was suddenly there in front of Ki. He had his fly unzipped and was bracing himself against the back wall of a second saloon.

"Hey—" That was as far as he got. A turning kick caught him in the small of the back, sending him crashing into the wall. A second kick smashed into his windpipe, and the outlaw stayed down.

With cold-numbed fingers Ki set his second charge within a few feet of the outlaw's body, behind a stack of empty crates. Three minutes . . . He lit the fuse and got the hell out of there.

From the other end of town a shout went up and Ki silently cursed. Jessie and Dancer had been discovered. And if they were caught and detained . . .

Dancer had no choice. He drew his revolver and fired three times into the fat man's body. Jessica had slipped the wire holding the corral gate fast, and the fat man had appeared from out of the blizzard to grab her arm, turn her, and slap her.

160

Dancer's bullets punched through his body. The first, through the shoulder, turned him; the second found heart and lungs, and the fat man went down in the snow.

The bullets had started the horses running, and now they galloped through the open gate, narrowly missing Jessica as they rushed away from the man-sound of Dancer's Colt.

"Come on, for Christ's sake!" Dancer shouted. Jessica, snatching up her sack of explosives, ran through the snow to join him. A second outlaw appeared out of the stable, gun ready. Dancer's was first. A spinning .44 slug ripped into the thug's throat and sent him back into the stable, his blood spattering the snow with crimson.

Jessie and Ki darted down an alley. Behind them there was a shout, but no mass pursuit. The storm had muffled the shots just enough.

"Here!" Dancer said, halting behind the hotel, which was little more than a mass flophouse for the outlaws; single-storied, smelling of men and grime even from the outside. There couldn't be much time left. They set two charges and got the hell out of there.

"A minute, two?" Jessie panted.

"Call it one. Finish it off here," Dancer said. The remaining charges were fused and lit. Dancer heaved one on top of a nearby, unidentifiable building. Jessie tossed hers ahead of them in the alley—there was no time left for selecting targets—and they ran for it up a gentle, wooded slope behind the town. The first blast knocked Jessica from her feet, face down in the snow. She felt Dancer grab her arm and yank her upright and they ran on, Jessica's head buzzing, her knees wobbly.

By the time the second blast thundered through the day, shaking the snow from the pines around them, they were out of sight from the town and they could turn, leaning together, and watch their demonic work.

The hotel flew into the air in a mass of fluttering siding and shingles which swirled through the snowy sky before settling to burn. Men staggered from buildings below, some of them half naked, dazed.

"Ki," Jessica panted, but there was no telling if Ki was

safe or not. If he had been caught... Another blast, this one from the north end of town caused a saloon to lift slightly from its foundations and then slowly tilt forward and collapse in the street.

It too was soon burning. Jessica saw a man below them lift an accusing finger in their direction and start forward with three outlaws following. The charge in the alley went off just then, blowing them into the air. When they landed they didn't move. One man's leg lay a good distance from the rest of his body.

Horses stampeded through the street. The flames, eerie through the mask of snow, illuminated strangely the chaos below. Half of the town was destroyed or burning. The outlaws milled around in numbed confusion.

"There he is!" Jessica shouted, pulling away from Dancer. Then he too could see Ki racing toward them through the snow, weaving through the trees.

He reached them, exhausted, breathing raggedly, glowing with pleasure. "Now—let's get the hell out of here!" he said, and they started northward, toward Yoshiko and their horses, with the crackle of flames and the cries of pain in their ears, the snow around them still reflecting the crimson sheets of flames rising from the destroyed outlaw town.

It was an exhausting walk northward, but three hours later they still saw no one on their backtrail, and they found Yoshiko just where they had sent her.

Ki shook his head in happy disbelief as the girl rushed to meet him. "So, you have finally obeyed me," Ki said, and as he stroked her hair there was genuine pleasure, genuine fondness in his voice.

"You do love me," Yoshiko said happily.

"I am pleased to see you, pleased that you are here and safe," Ki said, but if Yoshiko noticed the difference in Ki's perception of things she gave no indication of it. She simply clung to him more tightly.

The horses were rested, if hungry, and Dancer had already led them forward. Jessica mounted and looked down the trail once again as Ki disentangled himself from Yoshiko's arms. Jessie's borrowed gray horse was long gone. That left them one short, but Yoshiko had no objection to climbing up behind Ki, holding him around the waist, resting her head against his back as they discussed things.

"They'll be more alert than ever in the passes, Ki," Dancer said. "I doubt we'll be able to slip out like we did last time."

"No," Ki agreed, "there's very little chance that way, but it doesn't matter; we're not going west, toward Beaverton."

"Grand Forks?"

"That's right. I could be wrong, but I don't think so. That is where King has gone to complete his transactions."

"Still think he'll try to buy Centennial?"

"Even if he doesn't," Jessica said correctly, "he's a millionaire for his efforts. If Ki's right, he's got everything stashed away in the Grand Forks bank. He'll be off for San Francisco or who-knows-where, fat and wealthy. Or so he thinks."

"So he thinks," Ki agreed. "We'll go west, over the hills. With luck we won't meet any sentries in that direction. With luck we'll reach Grand Forks not far behind the marshal. It is time," he added soberly, "that we became the hunters."

Chapter 17

There was nothing particularly grand about Grand Forks. It lay between the southern and western forks of the Comstock River on the western slope of the mountains. From above, it looked well-organized, tidy, and picturesque, with the new snow gleaming in the early morning sunlight. Inside the town, however, it was a bog of mud and slush, with unpainted buildings crowding a deeply rutted main street.

Ki, Jessica, Dancer, and Yoshiko rode into the town at eight that morning with the cold wind at their backs. Their horses, breath steaming from their nostrils, dragged a little with weariness. The bank wasn't open yet, and so they had their first real meal in a long while at the local restaurant.

"If the bank is involved," Dancer asked, "how are we ever going to prove it?"

"There are ways," Jessica answered. "I'll bring my own examiner in if I have to. If they don't have anything to hide, they'll probably let me look at the books now."

"You? Why would they?"

"You really don't know what the name Starbuck means," Ki put in. "They'll let Jessie have her look—if there isn't something crooked going on."

"If you have to bring someone in and get a warrant and so forth it will take a long time. Too damn long. King can be gone by then."

"King is not going anywhere," Ki promised. "Not if I have to hold him here by main force."

"Assuming he's in town at all." Dancer poked at his

164

cold eggs. "This whole thing could be a wild-goose chase, you know."

No one answered him. They knew that as well as Michael Dancer did. The trip to Grand Forks was based on several assumptions, nothing more. The name on the filing cabinet—Ki admitted to himself that it could have come from anywhere. The knowledge that the silver pirates would have needed some help in trading the silver for currency. The assumption that King wouldn't return to Beaverton at this point, and that Grand Forks was the nearest town of any size. None of that made for certainty, but Ki still would have bet that King was in town.

The trick was to find him and hold him until they could scratch up the proof they needed that he was involved in a dozen murders, in the robberies and in a basketful of other crimes.

"He killed Jack Troupe," Dancer said.

"Sure. He knew through the telegraph office that an investigator was on the way from San Francisco. He didn't want anyone around poking into what was going on at Centennial." Jessie leaned back in her chair, finishing her coffee.

Ki suggested, "You got away with it for a while, Dancer, because you were undercover. As soon as they figured out who you were you were a marked man. You undoubtedly would have been lynched by an angry mob."

"If not for you. You and Jessica also had to go."

"They made their try; we were lucky."

Yoshiko sat looking at them, listening perhaps, or perhaps dreaming. Ki glanced at her and thought of Kobi-san. The Master. He still wanted to kill Ki, would if he had the chance, and there seemed to be nothing Ki could do about it. Kobi-san would not listen. His mind had been made up. It was a matter of honor.

Sooner or later one of them had to die.

Jessica stretched and said, "How about checking in with the local law?"

"Is that a good idea?" Dancer asked.

"We might get some help. It can't hurt."

"No? With King being a brother officer and all?"

"Most lawmen would want to be the first to put a bad one away," Ki commented.

Dancer just shrugged. His experience with local lawmen hadn't been that good. But after breakfast they walked across the street, Yoshiko in tow, to talk to the town marshal, whose name was Gladden.

He knew Jessica on sight.

Ben Gladden was nearly six-foot-four, and must have weighed about a hundred and seventy pounds. He smoked a corncob pipe with deep relish and blew smoke out his nostrils the whole time he spoke to Jessie.

"Damn me! Sure I recall you. Alex Starbuck gave me my first job as a sailor before I went crazy and took up the law as a living. I don't 'spect you'd know me now, Jessie, but you haven't changed much since you were twelve, thirteen. Pretty as always. Now, what brings you down to this mudhole of ours?"

Jessica told Gladden and he listened quietly, nodding his head once in a while, lighting his pipe twice. "I know Eric King," he said at last. "Never thought he was much of a lawman, but this is hard to take. Can hardly believe it."

"It's the truth," Dancer put in. The marshal glanced at the tall young man perched on his desk and nodded.

"I 'spect it is if Jessica Starbuck says it. That's different from proving it, though." The marshal shook his head. "Ma, I always want to see the proof. Like to think I never hung an innocent man."

"That's why we want to see the bank records," Jessica said.

The marshal puffed at his pipe again. "I don't see why that can't be managed. If Howard Pickett isn't willing to open up the books, I'll have the judge open 'em for us."

Ki said, "I'd like to know if King is in town first."

"So would I," Gladden agreed. "I'll have someone check out the hotel and the boarding houses. If he's using his own name, which isn't likely, we'll dig him up and have a talk with him. There's also the chance he's staying at a private house." The lawman shrugged. "We'll have a try at it and see if we can't turn King up. It'd be interesting to talk to him. You're sure he's here, are you?"

"It's a reasonable conjecture," Ki said. The marshal's eyebrows slid up but he said nothing in response.

"When does the bank open?" Jessica asked.

Gladden swiveled in his chair and glanced at the brass-bound clock on the wall. "They should be unlocking right about now. Why don't we saunter on over and see what we can find out."

It was two muddy blocks to the bank and when they reached it they found a bemused bespectacled man standing on the plankwalk, looking hard at his gold pocket watch.

"What's up, Erwin?" the lawman asked. He explained to the others, "Erwin here's the bank teller."

Erwin tucked his watch away, glanced haughtily at Ki and Dancer, and said, "It's still locked, and it's past nine." He toe tapped impatiently. "I can't understand this. This has never happened. Mr. Pickett is quite punctilious."

"Break in," Ki suggested immediately. Marshal Gladden thought it over for a moment and nodded. The teller objected, but it did him no good. Ki and the marshal shouldered the door in and walked into the empty bank.

The nearly empty bank.

The dead man lay behind the counter in front of an open safe. Papers were strewn about the floor. A single close-range gunshot wound in the chest had done the job.

Ki crouched down and examined the body. "Howard Pickett?" he asked, although there wasn't much doubt that the balding fat man was the bank president.

"It's him," Gladden answered.

The bank teller had gone a funny shade of green. Leaning back against the counter, he made a gurgling noise in his throat as he looked at death for the first time in his young life.

"Anything missing here?" the marshal asked.

The teller stammered as he answered, "I'd have to look."

"Do it, dammit."

"It won't be there," Jessica said, as the teller, avoiding the dead man, looked through the open safe. "Any evidence as to what was going on will be gone. King is a lot of things, but he hasn't shown himself to be a fool yet."

"There's just the special account book missing," the teller, crouched on his heels, said. "A blue and gold book with our favored clients' transactions listed."

"That'll be it," Ki guessed.

"No sense looking through the hotels for him now," Gladden said. "He's gone."

"Which way?" Jessica wondered.

"There's no way of telling," Ki answered. "Certainly not back toward Beaverton. All we can do now is spread out and try to find someone who might have seen him riding out of town."

Gladden looked again at the dead man, shook his head, and agreed. "I'll round up some help. I'll send someone over for the body, Erwin."

"What am I supposed to do?" the teller wanted to know. "I mean . . . what am I supposed to do!"

"That's up to you, I 'spect. Lock up or open for business, whatever you want. I've got other things on my mind."

"Ki?" Jessica was crouched near the safe. When she straightened up she held out her hand. A five-pointed star was in it, the pin bent. Ki glanced at the marshal who nodded and spat.

"Let's find him," Gladden said.

Outside, Ki stopped Yoshiko and turned her toward him. "Now this is what you will do. Go find the hotel and get a room. Lie down and sleep for as long as you can."

"Ki . . ."

"There is now a safe place to leave you. You will stay," he said, and his tone of voice left no doubt about his seriousness.

She looked into his eyes and finally nodded. "As you wish. You will be back for me?"

"I will be back,"

Yoshiko started off up the street, head bowed, and Ki

ran to catch up with the others. Gladden was talking. ". . . coroner. You three scratch around and see what you can find out. When my deputy comes in, I'll send him out as well."

Ki took the stable but had no luck there. An old man sitting on a chair in the sunshine in the center of town was either deaf or pretended to be. Passersby had no time for his questions. It was Jessie who found the kid with the shock of flaming red hair playing ball in an alley.

"He remembered King because he had a red mustache. He's riding a palomino, Ki, riding west. There were two other men with him."

"The marshal?" Dancer asked.

"No. I don't think we need the marshal just yet," Ki answered grimly.

In minutes they were mounted and out of town, following the three horsemen, whose trail was distinct in the new snow. In a stand of pines they lost the tracks and an hour's searching failed to pick them up again.

Jessica thought she knew where they were going. "There's a town called Tourmaline about ten miles ahead, Ki."

"I never heard of it," Dancer said.

"No reason to. It's not much of a place. Many years ago they had a fair-sized copper strike at Tourmaline, but it's long since dried up."

"Then why would King head there?"

"Ki, remember? There's a railroad spur there."

She was right, and Ki cursed himself for taking so long to think of that. In its heyday Tourmaline had wangled a railroad spur from the Colorado Eastern to haul copper ore to Denver. The copper was gone, but the railroad still stopped there.

"It has to be," Ki said. He lifted his eyes to the distance. They started on, quickly now, across snowfields where the sunny day was rapidly clearing patches of grass. It had to be Tourmaline. Once there King could strike out for Denver, and from there, anyplace in the country.

Things had gotten too hot for him to go ahead with the

169

original plan to ruin Centennial and then buy it out. No matter—he had a fortune already socked away, enough to live out his life in anyway he chose, and the hell with those who had died on his backtrail.

It was nearly sundown when they hit Tourmaline. Ki was leading the way as they rode into the tumble-down little mining town. Jessica lifted a pointing finger. "Ki!"

The train was in the station already, steam hissing from its release valves, the forebox glowing oddly in the sun-down light. They lifted their tired horses to a trot and reached the depot in time to hear the train's bell clang three times.

Jessica rushed to the window of the ticket office. "Three men, one of them with a red mustache, did they buy tickets?"

"Three men," the ticket clerk drawled, rubbing his jaw. "Let me see."

"You can't have that many passengers!"

"There was three, yeah. Not from hereabouts. Through tickets to Denver."

"Thank you." The train gave a loud sighing sound and the drive wheels clanked. Jessica waved frantically at Ki, pointing to the train. "Tickets," Jessica nearly shouted. "Three. Now."

"Lady, you ain't gonna make that train—"

"Now."

"Look here..." But the train was already gaining speed. Jessica turned in disgust from the ticket window, raced along the platform past a startled conductor, and leaped for the door of a Pullman car, gripping the handrails and pulling herself on board.

Breathing hard, she opened the door to the Pullman and looked through it to see Ki as the far end. Slowly Jessica walked down the aisle, seeing only four passengers, a mother and child, a drummer in a checked suit, and a sleeping cowboy.

"If we're wrong, it's a long ride to Denver," Ki said. He said it lightly, but there was concern behind his words. To lose King now would be heartbreaking.

"We're not wrong," Jessica said positively.

"Womanly intuition?"

"Call it what you like. He's on board this train."

Jessie couldn't have explained why she felt that way, why she *knew* the man was there. He was; that was all. Ki braced himself in the doorway as the train clattered around a long curve, wheels clacking, whistle blowing. Dancer appeared through the door of the Pullman, the rush of wind and sound accompanying him, causing eyes to lift.

"There's no one forward in the next car," he said.

"Sure?" Jessie asked.

"How could I miss Marshal King?"

"Then the car behind us," Jessie said. Ki accepted her premise. He teased Jessie about her so-called intuition from time to time, but she was right a lot more than she was wrong. The three of them made their way back through the car, Jessica using the backs of the aisle seats to brace herself as the train rattled on, picking up speed as it entered a long downward stretch of track.

"They aren't going to be happy to see you," Dancer said. He showed Jessica the pistol he was carrying beside his thigh.

She shook her head as Dancer offered her the gun. She was unarmed for the time being, but trusted to her two men. If they couldn't do the job between them, it wasn't going to get done.

Ki stepped between the cars and slid back the door to the next Pullman.

King was in the first aisle seat, legs stretched out, saddlebags on his lap. There was a man beside him and one across the aisle in the next row down. All of them were galvanized at the sight of the three hunters.

Dancer dove for King, but he was cut off by the man seated next to the marshal. Big, black-bearded, he leaped across King's legs and rushed up the aisle. Dancer tried to recover, but went to one knee. King kneed him in the face and Dancer was driven back into the wall.

Jessica lunged after the escaping bearded man and dragged him down by the ankles. He went down hard and when he tried to come to his hands and knees Jessie kicked him hard on the butt, driving him into the iron frame of the railroad seat before him. The man fell like a stunned ox.

King had leaped over the back of the seat he was in, carrying his saddlebags with him. Ki was right behind him, but as he reached out for the marshal, King swung around, gun in hand, and Ki had to dive for the floor as a .44 slug ripped through the seat above him.

The third man was on King's heels. Michael Dancer came up with his own revolver and touched off. The bullet tagged the bandit low on the left leg and he went down.

King was already out the door when Ki vaulted a seat to reach the aisle. The door let a rush of a coal-scented air into the interior of the Pullman as King went out. He turned again and fired through the glass half of the door, sending Ki to the floor again. Then the marshal was gone.

Ki glanced back at Jessica and Dancer and she waved him on. "I'm all right!" A conductor had burst into the car to find out what was happening and he too stood over the downed outlaw Jessica had taken out.

Ki went to the door low, moving cautiously. There was no sign of King out there. Had he jumped? Ki opened the door, sending broken glass to the floor, and went out.

The wind was cold and swift against his body. Behind him was the caboose, but the door was locked. Ki glanced upward. A ladder running to the roof of the Pullman was King's only possible escape route. Ki palmed a *shuriken* and started up.

Lifting his head up above the roof Ki drew another pair of shots from the marshal's .44 revolver. He could see King, briefly, on one knee, saddlebags beside him.

Ki shifted to the left and came up again, the throwing star humming from his hand. It missed. The train, swinging around a bend, swayed and clanked, tilting badly. The amazing part wasn't that Ki had missed, but that the *shuriken* had come so close to finishing the renegade marshal.

Ki clambered up as another bullet whined off the metalwork of the railroad coach and sang off into the distance. King tried another shot, but the hammer fell on an empty cylinder and he scrambled to his feet, running up the spine of the Pullman, as smoke and cinders drifted past him.

Beyond them the country was green grass and white patches of snow, gray skies with drifting clouds shadowing the land. Ki saw all of this only from the corners of his eyes. His attention was focused on the marshal, only on him.

King reached the break between the two Pullman cars and leaped across. Ki was on his heels and King knew it. He turned, hurled his pistol at Ki, and the, with his mouth open—maybe he was laughing, maybe gasping for air— he leaped from the train into space.

Ki saw the body hit the bank below them at thirty miles an hour, saw it twist and crumple and fold up. He was standing, watching the unmoving remains of King, as the train swept around another curve and entered the deep pine forest, rattling on toward Denver.

Ki bent, picked up the saddlebags the marshal had dropped, and started back down to meet Jessica.

Chapter 18

Dancer rolled Jessie over and she spread her legs, going to hands and knees as Dancer scooted against her, his solid shaft fitting the cleft of her body. For five long minutes he took her like that, took her slowly, gently, swaying with her own natural rhythm until she rolled onto her back without losing him, and smiling, beckoned him down to her, to meet her mouth with his, to press against her breasts as her legs lifted, spread, her heels hooking around his shoulders.

Dancer arched his back and braced himself, leaning back, his eyes taking in the lush sweep of Jessica Starbuck's body, lingering on the full, firm breasts and the pink buds of her nipples as he moved against her, his pace quickening, his skin flushing, his muscles standing out in relief as his body went taut from head to foot.

He went down to her again, hooking an arm around her neck, drawing her mouth to his, feeling the darting search of her tongue, the sweet clutching of her body against his shaft.

Jessica's forehead was beaded lightly with perspiration at the hairline. Her eyes were deep, distant, focused yet unfocused on Dancer as he thrust harder, deeper, working toward a hard, trembling climax.

After their lovemaking, Jessica dressed slowly, standing before the morning-lit window of the hotel room. Dancer, wearing only his trousers, watched. The trip back from Denver had been long and tiring, but each of them felt a satisfaction. The job was nearly complete, with only the loose ends to round up.

"How much did Ki say was in those saddlebags?" Dancer asked.

"Two hundred thousand," Jessica said, buttoning her blouse. "That leaves a lot of money unaccounted for; but you have to figure most of it drifted out of the territory in the pockets of the outlaws."

"Or was blown up by us at Castle Wells," Dancer said.

"That's possible too," Jessica agreed, tucking in her blouse, buttoning her jeans. She walked to Dancer, rumpled his hair, and kissed him once. Then she brushed her hair before the mirror, Dancer's fascinated eyes still on her.

"Where to this morning? The Centennial?"

"Yes. That's still got to be straightened out."

"Did you see Earl Gibbons last night?" he asked.

"Ki did. He went out with a new wagon and recovered the silver we left on the trail. He's supposed to go to Castle Wells today and see what else is left out there. There should be more bullion somewhere."

"The town have a marshal yet?"

"No. Temporarily a man named Crawford is filling in, but there'll be an election in a few days."

Dancer swung out of his chair and walked to Jessica, holding her tight, his hands cupping the softness of her breasts. "You haven't had enough?" she teased.

"Never." He grew thoughtful. "Has Ki found a way to get rid of Yoshiko yet?"

"What makes you sure he wants to?"

"The woman's too damned serious—and too young."

"He hasn't told me a thing," Jessie said, putting on her hat and adjusting the drawstring.

"I wish I'd seen King go down," Dancer said. There was anger in his words. "That bastard ruined a lot of lives."

"And nearly got you hung."

"That too. I just wish I'd seen him go off the train."

"Brighten up, Michael Dancer. King's gone; most of the money's back where it belongs. You've done your job."

"Yeah," Dancer muttered. He wasn't looking forward to going back to San Francisco. Unlike Ki he was in no hurry to get rid of his lady. He tugged on his shirt and boots as Jessica stood at the open window, watching two mockingbirds squabble their way across the sky.

Ki wasn't in his room when they went to check on him; nor was he downstairs in the restaurant. Yoshiko was nowhere around either. It didn't matter—they didn't need Ki to do what had to be done. Presumably he was trying to straighten out his personal entanglement.

Jessie and Dancer rode out to the mine, meeting Strangfeld at the front gate of Centennial. The big man didn't look as unhappy as he normally did; in fact, he nearly smiled as Jessica swung down from her horse's back.

"Mornin', boss," Strangfeld said.

"Good morning. How are things going?"

"Funny thing is," the mine manager said, walking with them to the office, "things are going well enough. I never thought sitting down and talking with these people would do any good. Men were too damn mad, you know. But it seemed to do some good, and then when the news came through that the tiger gang had been broken up, that King was behind it all with some hired whites and some Japs this Takahashi character had hired, it seemed to make us all stop and look at each other and realize that we'd been damn fools."

The mine was busy, a full crew working. Dancer pointed out that every man he saw was white.

"Yeah, I know," Strangfeld said. "That was a temporary fix we came up with at the meeting. For the time being, until everyone has time to cool down, I've got all the whites on one shift, all the Japanese on another. It ain't something that'll last, but they thought it might help. It's an idea they come up with themselves at the meeting, so maybe while things settle back to normal it's the best thing."

"The pay scale?" Jessica asked as they walked across the muddy yard.

"That's cleared up, boss. I really blew it on that one, I guess. At the time it seemed like the easiest way to go. Give the bookkeeper time to get things organized. I was wrong." Strangfeld stopped, wiped his forehead with a red kerchief and replaced his hat. "But some of us are slow to learn. I guess I'm one of 'em. Things are getting back to normal, anyway—I heard some of the boys talk about going down to the shantytown and helping the Japs rebuild some of their houses." He shrugged. "That alone lets you hope that things are going to blow over, and that everybody's back to thinking straight."

"It's hard," Jessica said, "when you think someone's taking your livelihood away. Maybe now we can all get back to work." She laughed, "And I can get out of your hair."

"Well, I wasn't real happy with you showing up, lady —Miss Starbuck—but it's obvious now I was losing control and didn't even realize it. What can you say? I done my best, but it wasn't good enough."

After a quick inspection of the mine, Dancer and Jessica rode back to town. The day was clear but cool, with a light breeze out of the north.

The temporary marshal was waiting in the doorway to meet them as they hitched their ponies.

"How are you, Mr. Crawford?" Jessica asked, offering the new marshal her hand. He was a mournful-looking man in a dark suit and derby. His hound-dog eyes stared out at the world unhappily.

"Doin' all right, I expect. I just wish they'd have that election and let me go back to my butcher shop." Crawford inclined his head. "Come on in."

Dancer asked drily, "Sure you're not going to lock me up? An escaped murderer?"

"No." Crawford sat at the desk uneasily. "But you can have you wallet back. Found an Indian named Jack Oaktree who admitted he'd lifted it from you at the hotel and took it out to Troupe's grave. King gave him five bucks for it."

"The Indian?" Jessica asked.

"I didn't hold him. Waste of time. The man just wanted some whisky money."

Jessie thought that the town could do worse than elect Crawford marshal, although he didn't seem to want the job.

"I got to write all these reports for the council," Crawford said wearily. "Waste of time. I could walk over and tell 'em in five minutes what went on here. Went out to Castle Wells— got your pistol here, young lady, by the way—beautiful weapon. Found a wagon load of silver bullion. It's on its way back to Strangfeld. Found quite a few bodies, but no live bandits. Know anything about how those men were killed?" Crawford asked while he squinted at Jessica.

"Probably a falling-out," Dancer guessed.

"Yeah, probably. That seemed like the way the report should read . . . unless you two wanted to stay around for all of the legal rigmarole that's going to be coming up while our local politicians jockey for position. No? I didn't think so." He scribbled something on a yellow notepad. "A falling-out among the outlaws. Okay. I've got a man named Irv Dawson back there, the one you took off the Denver train. He's going to tell everything he knows with the hope of getting his neck out of the noose it's in." Crawford leaned back in his chair, his thumbs hooked in his belt. "He seems to think your Japanese friend killed Eric King."

"Eric King commited suicide," Jessica said. "He jumped from the train to avoid arrest."

"You'll swear to that?"

"Certainly."

"Good enough," Crawford said, tilting forward again. "I guess we've got nothing else to talk about. If I can speak for the town, I appreciate what you three did here. We all do."

"That's that, then," Dancer said as they went outside. The day was beginning to cloud over again, and to the north they could see faint gray curtains of rain. "It's over."

"You?" Jessica asked.

Dancer looped his arm around her waist. "San Francisco. Unless . . ." He shrugged, knowing that what they had was beautiful but temporary. There was a man somewhere in the depths of Jessica Starbuck's heart. Who he might be or what might have gone on between them Dancer couldn't guess. But he knew there was a man. One man—one he couldn't contend with.

"We'll be going soon," Jessie said hastily. She looked away from Dancer, her sea-green eyes on the distant clouds. "As soon as Ki is ready."

And where was Ki now? This wasn't like him—to take off without saying a word. *Where was Ki?*

The mountains stood out like dark etchings against a gray sky. Higher up, there was snow. The rain drifted up the long valley. Ki stood with his arm around Yoshiko. Now she must understand. Now she must be told so that she knew how things must be.

"My warrior," she said, looking up into his eyes. "We—"

Ki's voice wasn't sharp, but it was firm. "There is no 'we,' Yoshiko. You and I cannot walk the same path again."

"Ki! We made love and touched deeply and spoke together of life and our souls." The eyes were astonished, hurt, questioning.

"We touched, and it was good," Ki said. "But now it has ended. Once we were like brother and younger sister. Now we have been lovers. Both were good times, the best of times, but now they are gone."

"Ki . . ." Her eyes showed sudden panic. She gripped Ki's shirt tightly with both hands. The oak tree hovering over them creaked in the wind. "We cannot end."

"We have ended." Ki looked away deliberately. It was painful to do this to Yoshiko, but she had to be made to understand finally.

She said nothing. She kept her head down as her hands fell away. She recognized the finality in his tone.

"I want you to go home," Ki said to her back. "To go there with Kobi-san. Decide what you wish to do with your life. I cannot be a part of it."

She still would not lift her head. She made no gesture, uttered no word. An especially strong gust of wind rippled through the branches of the oak and sent a chill up Ki's spine.

He knew.

Ki turned slowly, his body tensing, heart beginning to race as adrenaline coursed through his body. The Master was there.

Kobi-san came forward silently, like a leaf on the wind, his robes flowing, his ancient eyes piercing beneath the white brows, his arms folded, his body like a cat's body: springy, deceptively lazy. He moved hear to Ki and looked up at him, bowing.

"It is time, Ki, deceiver."

Yoshiko turned now, her eyes anguished, her mouth slightly open. She started forward and then stopped as if warned off by the nearly palpable menace she saw in the eyes of her grandfather, the determination in the dark eyes of Ki, her love, her samurai.

"There is no need to fight, Kobi-san," Ki said softly as the Master's arms unfolded, his legs flexing slightly. "The woman is ready now to go with you. There is nothing between us."

"You have betrayed your trust, Ki. You may not live."

"Master, what has been has been, and now it is past. To carry the past with us is slow death. Go and live out your days in peace. I am the younger man, the stronger man. I have no wish to hurt you. I love you like a father still."

"I loved you like a son, Ki, but when the whelp is evil, the wolf must kill it before it harms itself and others."

"Ki! Kobi-san!" Yoshiko cried out. But neither man paid any attention to her; their eyes were on each other, measuring the readiness of muscle and sinew, the stance, the eyes which signaled an attack.

"You are younger, Ki, stronger perhaps, but there are movements you never learned, had no time to learn, which take a lifetime to learn. I could kill you now. I will do it, for it must be done or the monastery is shamed forever."

Ki wanted to discuss it still, to argue, to plead if necessary, but there was no talking to Kobi-san now. He was fixed on his one idea—to kill Ki, the evil.

Slowly the old man's arms spread wide and his robe dropped away from his back. Parchment-colored flesh covered the lean, still ropy muscles of the Master. He bowed to Ki and assumed the dragon stance.

Ki glanced at the sky, at Yoshiko, who stood horrified, watching. There was no running then, and no way to stop the Master except by killing him.

Ki closed his eyes briefly in meditation. Then his own body coiled into his chosen stance, the tiger position more suited to defense than attack.

The master was old, wispy, tiny compared to Ki, but his

180

first sharp attack was enough to kill a man who did not know the ways of *te*.

The *yonhon-nukite* blow, deadly and powerful, just short of Ki's heart, seemed a probing thrust. Ki reflexively blocked it with a *gedan-barai*, his crossed wrists turning the deadly blow aside as he turned his body.

Kobi-san grunted, perhaps with satisfaction. The student had not forgotten everything then, he seemed to say silently.

The Master turned, sidekicked, had that attack blocked by Ki's slapping hand, and spun to the other foot, his heel this time striking beneath Ki's defense, cracking against his unguarded ribs.

Ki backed away, pain flooding his side. He had never been in a situation like this, one which required only defense. He could not, would not strike back, but to be forever defensive in *te* was to lose.

The Master, hand turned up, struck at Ki's forehead with a *nakadate*, or middle-knuckle punch, and Ki ducked away, feeling the astonishingly powerful blow glance off his temple, lighting brilliant flares in his head. Before he had recovered from that the Master kicked again at him, this blow landing on Ki's kneecap, nearly snapping the leg.

Ki slapped the next spinning kick away, and backing from the Master, reacted too slowly to a *choku-zuki* blow, which grazed his throat, briefly strangling Ki's breath off.

Still, Ki felt in control of the situation. The Master was an old man. He wasn't simply going through his forms now; he was putting all he had behind his blows, and he was bound to tire if only Ki could hold him off, preventing that one chop or kick which could disable or kill.

"Fight, Ki," the Master said breathily. "Do not give me your life; make me take it."

"I will not fight you, Master," Ki said.

"Then you will die, Ki. Then you will die."

What happened next was something Ki had never encountered or dreamed of. He was, after all, a *te* master in his own right. His hands and feet had defeated some of the best in the world, strong vigorous, younger men: the Iceman, the Destroyer—huge and powerful men had fallen to Ki's skills.

This was something different, something he had never seen, a lesson from the Master.

He was smoke swirling around Ki, but his hands, feet, elbows, and knees were thrusting iron. Honed steel chopped at Ki's neck and all of Ki's defenses were negated by the twisting, brutal adderlike strokes of Kobi-san.

Ki felt his wind go as he fought back futilely against a thrust such as he had ever seen. Kobi-san's arm seemed to loop out of nowhere and touch Ki's midsection with a crushing blow that threatened to stop his heart.

Ki fell back, every instinct in his body demanding that he fight back, his mind arguing against it.

"Now you will have your final lesson, Ki, traitor," Kobi-san said. He moved in again, a dervish armed with swordlike arms which chopped against Ki's body and head, driving the *te* disciple to the ground as the Master hovered over him, tall, wispy, indomitable.

A kick narrowly missed Ki's head. He managed to block the next sidekick but could not catch the foot at the ankle. The master's other foot thudded into Ki's neck and sent him sprawling.

The rain fell down now. The great oak was a black shadow against the gray skies beyond. The Master was over him, and he would kill now. Ki could do nothing about it except strike out with his own killing blows, and he would not do that.

The Master feinted with one thrust. Then the left hand, twisting, the middle knuckle driving for Ki's throat, slipped past the samurai's defenses.

Yoshiko screamed and the world went black, as the cold rain continued to fall.

Chapter 19

He was dead. The old man was dead, lying on his back against the cold damp grass as the young Japanese woman knelt over him, her hair loose, her body tense with anguish.

Ki rose slowly from the ground to walk toward them. Yoshiko shreiked, "Get away for him! Do you hear? Get away!"

Ki nodded and backed off a little. He stood trying to catch his breath beneath the oak. The driving rain obscured the land now, the mountains becoming formless shadows, the valleys ghostly depressions.

Dead, Kobi-san was dead.

He had been ready to administer the killing stroke to Ki's throat when he straightened up, clutched at his heart and staggered backward to fall against the ground, his body twitching. Moments later he was dead, the anger washed out of his eyes.

"You killed him," Yoshiko said, lifting her face to the rain.

"It was no one's fault. He was an old man who exerted himself too much," Ki said. "It was his heart."

"You killed him," she repeated, resting her cheek against the Master's still chest.

They remained like that for a long while as the wind blew and the rain slanted down. Finally Ki touched her arm. "We must go now, Yoshiko."

"Go where you please," she said, tearing her arms from his grip.

"No. Now we go together. To town, to find someone to take the body."

"I will not have it buried here. It must go to Japan."

"Then we will see what can be done about that." Ki looked into her eyes. The old emotions were gone, replaced by a coldness, a deadness of spirit. Now the game was gone; now death had hit close to Yoshiko and she knew there was no such thing as an immortal man. Not her samurai, not Kobi-san, the Master himself.

Now Yoshiko allowed Ki to help her to her feet, and together they walked back toward Beaverton, the girl stumbling a little as they went. "I am going home now," she said once. "Now you have your wish, Ki. I am going home, taking Grandfather to the monastery—and there I will remain."

She left Ki at the town limits, a lonely, tiny figure walking away through the rain. She didn't want his help with what had to be done now. The game was over, the dream done. There was no place suddenly for a samurai in her life.

Ki was packing away the few new clothes he had bought when Jessica Starbuck came into his hotel room. He turned toward her slowly, shrugged, and returned to his work, folding a shirt with meticulous care.

"I just found out, Ki. I'm sorry."

"It was a tragic thing," he answered without turning.

"Your teacher, your *father*."

"It is over, Jessie," Ki said, in a way that indicated he didn't want to pursue the subject any further.

"All right. I'm just about finished packing too, Ki. We can leave when you want to."

"Dancer?" he asked.

"Dancer's gone already. San Francisco."

That was a subject Jessica didn't care to discuss just then. She left Ki to his packing and returned to her own room. Like Ki she had only a few new things since the fire at the other hotel. These were already packed. There was only her hat on the bed, her gunbelt on the bedside table, her jacket.

She stood at the window a moment as she put on her hat, looking out at Beaverton. It seemed that the town would survive after all, continuing as long as the mine did, perhaps even outlasting it. Who knew?

At the sound of footsteps on the floorboards Jessica turned, thinking it was the bellhop for her luggage.

The ghost stood there, the thing risen from the dead.

He took a step forward and then halted, his gun in hand. Marshal King's face was battered, his clothing torn. When he walked, there was a terrible limp to his right leg. His left arm hung uselessly at his side.

"You little bitch," he hissed between broken teeth.

"Alive?" Jessica said in wonder, backing up a step.

King took three painfully slow steps forward. The hammer on his Remington revolver was drawn back, his finger wrapped around its trigger.

"Alive, yeah. Crippled up. Broke, on the run. All thanks to you, you nosy, meddling bitch. I had it all. Enough money to live out three lifetimes. I could have gone on forever, milking the Centennial. But you had to come and destroy it all. You'll pay now," he said hoarsely. "You'll pay for it now, you prying bitch."

She glanced toward the bedside table where her .38 revolver rested, but it was too far, just out of reach. King was keeping back far enough so that she had no chance to move in on him either. She could do nothing but take the bullet he had marked with her name.

"Jessica—"

Ki came in the door and then flung himself to one side as King, spinning, triggered off a round from his pistol, the bullet smashing into the plaster where Ki's head had been.

Jessica dove to her right, hand stretching out for the .38 on the table. King swung back toward her and fired wildly, his shot shattering the glass of the bedroom window.

Jessie's shot wasn't so poorly aimed. From a seated position she two-handed her pistol and fired twice, driving King back into the wall, where he stood up straight and then slowly slid to the floor, streaking the wall with blood.

She sat there a long while, still holding the pistol in

firing position until Ki rose, checked the body, and walked to her to help her to her feet.

"Dead. There's no doubt this time. It's over in Beaverton, Jessica. Finally over."

Watch for

**LONE STAR AND THE CHEYENNE
TRACKDOWN**

Sixty-seventh novel in the exciting
LONE STAR
series from Jove

coming in March!